Too Stup

"Your material is fabulous! It rem
Gemini Rising

Jane Smith's Translation Dictionary of Everyday Lies, Insults, Manipulations, and Clueless Comments

"Oooh, awesome!" C. Osborne

The ReGender App

"This book is brilliant. .... The scene at the airport had me laughing out loud. ..." Katya, Goodreads

"A book I really recommend to any book club and to people who are interested in gender differences and gender discrimination." Mesca Elin, Psychromatic Redemption

License to Do That

"I'm very much intrigued by the issues raised in this narrative. I also enjoy the author's voice, which is unapologetically combative but also funny and engaging." A.S.

"I love Froot Loup! You make me laugh out loud all the time!" Celeste M.

"A thought-provoking premise and a wonderful cast of characters." rejection letter from publisher

The Blasphemy Tour

"With plenty of humor and things to think about throughout, *The Blasphemy Tour* is a choice pick ...." *Midwest Book Review*

"Jass Richards has done it again. As I tell anyone who wants to listen, Jass is a comedy genius, she writes the funniest books and always writes the most believable unbelievable characters and scenes. ... I knew this book was a winner when ... a K9 unit dog kind of eats their special brownies ... and dances Thriller. ... Rev and Dylan are not your ordinary guy and girl protagonists with sexual tension and a romantic interest, at all. They both defy gender roles, and they are so smart and opinionated, it's both funny and made me think at the same time. ... They tour around the USA, in their lime green bus that says 'There are no gods. Deal with it.' Overall, I highly recommend anything by Jass, especially this one book, which is full of comedy gold and food for thought." May Arend, Brazilian Book Worm

"If I were Siskel and Ebert I would give this book Two Thumbs Way Up. ... Yes, it is blasphemy toward organized religion but it gives you tons of Bible verses to back up its premises. And besides, it's pure entertainment. There's a prequel which I recommend you read first. *The Road Trip Dialogues*. ... I only hope there will be a third book." L.K. Killian

"Wretchedly funny." C. Mike Rice, Realworldatheism.com

The Road Trip Dialogues

"I am impressed by the range from stoned silliness to philosophical perspicuity, and I love your comic rhythm." L. S.

"This is engaging, warm, funny work, and I enjoyed what I read. ..." rejection letter from publisher

"Just thought I'd let you know I'm on the Fish'n'Chips scene and laughing my ass off." Ellie Burmeister

"These two need stable jobs. Oh wait, no. Then we wouldn't get any more road trips. Fantastic book which expands the mind in a laid back sort of way. Highly recommended." lindainalabama

"Watched *Monty Python and the Holy Grail* last weekend. Could only think of Jass Richards and *The Road Trip Dialogues* ...." May Arend, Brazilian Book Worm

Dogs Just Wanna Have Fun

"Funny and entertaining! I looked forward to picking up this book at the end of a long day." Mary Baluta

"... terrifically funny and ingeniously acerbic ...." Dr. Patricia Bloom, My Magic Dog

"... laugh-out-loud funny." M.W., Librarything

This Will Not Look Good on My Resume

"Ya made me snort root beer out my nose!" Moriah Jovan, *The Proviso*

"Darkly humorous." Jennifer Colt, *The Hellraiser of the Hollywood Hills*

"HYSTERICAL! ... There are really no words to describe how funny this book is. ... Really excellent book." Alison, Goodreads

"This book is like a roller coaster ride on a stream of consciousness. ... Altogether, a funny, quirky read ...." Grace Krispy, Motherlode: Book Reviews and Original Photography

"Brett has trouble holding down a job. Mainly because she's an outspoken misanthrope who is prone to turn a dead-end job into a social engineering experiment. Sometimes with comically disastrous results, sometimes with comically successful results. (Like pairing up a compulsive shopper with a kleptomaniac for an outing at the mall.) I don't agree with everything she says, but I will defend her right to say it — because she's hilarious!

"My favorite part was when she taught a high school girls' sex ed class that 70% of boys will lie to get sex, 80% won't use a condom, yet 90% are pro-life. She was reprimanded, of course. I think she should have gotten a medal.

"You will likely be offended at one point or another, but if you are secure enough to laugh at your own sacred cows instead of just everyone else's, this is a must read." weikelm, Librarything

"Wonderful read, funny, sarcastic. Loved it!" Charlie, Smashwords

"I just loved this book. It was a quick read, and left me in stitches. ... " Robin McCoy-Ramirez

"First, let me just say I was glad I was not drinking anything while reading this. I refrained from that. My husband said he never heard me laugh so much from reading a book. At one point, I was literally in tears. Jass Richards is brilliant with the snappy comebacks and the unending fountain of information she can spout forth. ... The quick wit, the sharp tongue, the acid words and sarcasm that literally oozes from her pores ... beautiful." M. Snow, My Chaotic Ramblings

A Philosopher, a Psychologist, and an Extraterrestrial Walk into a Chocolate Bar

"Jass Richards is back with another great book that entertains and informs as she mixes feminism, critical thinking, and current social issues with humour ... The wedding intervention was hilarious. ...." James M. Fisher, *The Miramichi Reader*

"I found myself caught between wanting to sit and read [*A Philosopher, a Psychologist, and an Extraterrestrial Walk into a Chocolate Bar*] all in one go and wanting to spread it out. I haven't laughed that hard and gotten to spend time with such unflinchingly tough ideas at the same time. ... [And] the brilliance of the Alices! ... I can now pull out your book every time somebody tries to claim that novels can't have meaningful footnotes and references. [Thanks too] for pointing me to the brilliant essay series 'Dudes are Doomed.' I am eagerly watching for *The ReGender App* ...." C. Osborne

TurboJetslams: Proof #29 of the Non-Existence of God

"Extraordinarily well written with wit, wisdom, and laugh-out-loud ironic recognition, *TurboJetslams: Proof #29 of the Non-Existence of God* is a highly entertaining and a riveting read that will linger on in the mind and memory long after the little book itself has been finished and set back upon the shelf (or shoved into the hands of friends with an insistence that they drop everything else and read it!). Highly recommended for community library collections, it should be noted for personal reading lists." *Midwest Book Review*

"We all very much enjoyed it—it's funny and angry and heartfelt and told truly ... " McSweeney's

"If you're looking for a reading snack that has zero saccharine but is loaded with just the right combination of snark, sarcasm, and humor, you've found it." Ricki Wilson, Amazon

"What Richards has done is brilliant. At first, I began getting irritated as I read about a familiar character, or a familiar scenario from our time living on the lake. Then, as the main character amps up her game, I see the thrill in the planning and the retribution she undertakes for pay back." mymuskoka.blog spot.ca/2016/07/book-review-turbojetslams.html

Substitute Teacher from Hell

"I enjoyed reading 'Supply Teacher from Hell' immensely and found myself bursting out laughing many, many times. It is extremely well-written, clever, and very intelligent in its observations." Iris Turcott, dramaturge

more at
jassrichards.com

•

Writing as Peg Tittle

Jess

"[Jess'] perspective on being a girl and woman while having memories of being a man offers an understanding I'd never thought of. Really interesting book." Poolays, LibraryThing

Gender Fraud: a fiction

"A gripping read ...." Katya, Goodreads

Impact

"Edgy, insightful, terrific writing, propelled by rage against rape. Tittle writes in a fast-paced, dialogue-driven style that hurtles the reader from one confrontation to the next. Chock full of painful social observations ...." Hank Pellissier, Director of Humanist Global Charity

" ... The idea of pinning down the inflictors of this terror is quite appealing ...." Alison Lashinsky

It Wasn't Enough

"Unlike far too many novels, this one will make you think, make you uncomfortable, and then make you reread it ...." C. Osborne, moon speaker.ca

"... a powerful and introspective dystopia .... It is a book I truly recommend for a book club as the discussions could be endless ...." Mesca Elin, Goodreads

"Tittle's book hits you hard ...." D. Sohi, Goodreads

"*It Wasn't Enough* punches well above its weight and straight in the gut ...." Shefali Sequeira, 4w.pub

Exile

"Thought-provoking stuff, as usual from Peg Tittle." James M. Fisher, Goodreads

What Happened to Tom

"This powerful book plays with the gender gap to throw into high relief the infuriating havoc unwanted pregnancy can wreak on a woman's life. Once you've read *What Happened to Tom*, you'll never forget it." Elizabeth Greene, *Understories* and *Moving*

"I read this in one sitting, less than two hours, couldn't put it down. Fantastic allegorical examination of the gendered aspects of unwanted pregnancy. A must-read for everyone, IMO." Jessica, Goodreads

"Peg Tittle's *What Happened to Tom* takes a four-decades-old thought experiment and develops it into a philosophical novella of extraordinary depth and imagination .... Part allegory, part suspense (perhaps horror) novel, part defense of bodily autonomy rights (especially women's), Tittle's book will give philosophers and the philosophically minded much to discuss." Ron Cooper, *Hume's Fork*

Just Think about It!

"An excellent collection of thought-provoking essays and short pieces. *Just Think about It!* (2nd edn) covers an amazingly wide range of topics that really made me think ...." Karen Siddall, Amazon

Sexist Shit that Pisses Me Off

"Woh. This book is freaking awesome and I demand a sequel." Anonymous, barnesandnoble.com

"I recommend this book to both women and men. It will open your eyes to a lot of sexist—and archaic—behaviors." Seregon, Goodreads

"Honestly, selling this in today's climate is a daunting challenge— older women have grown weary, younger women don't seem to care, or at least don't really identify as feminists, men—forget that. All in all a sad state of affairs—sorry." rejection letter from agent

Shit that Pisses Me Off

"I find Peg Tittle to be a passionate, stylistically-engaging writer with a sharp eye for the hypocritical aspects of our society." George, Amazon

"Peg raises provocative questions: should people need some kind of license to have children? Should the court system use professional jurors? Many of her essays address the imbalance of power between men and women; some tackle business, sports, war, and the weather. She even explains why you're not likely to see Peg Tittle at Canada's version of an Occupy Wall Street demonstration. It's all thought-provoking, and whether or not you'll end up agreeing with her conclusions, her essays make for fascinating reading." Erin O'Riordan

"This was funny and almost painfully accurate, pointing out so many things that most of us try NOT to notice, or wish we didn't. Well written and amusing, I enjoyed this book immensely." Melody Hewson

" ... a pissed off kindred spirit who writes radioactive prose with a hint of sardonic wit .... Peg sets her sights on a subject with laser sharp accuracy then hurls words like missiles in her collection of 25 cogent essays on the foibles and hypocrisies of life .... Whether you agree or disagree with Peg's position on the issues, Shit that Pisses Me Off will stick to your brain long after you've ingested every word—no thought evacuations here. Her writing is adept and titillating ... her razor sharp words will slice and dice the cerebral jugular. If you enjoy reading smart, witty essays that challenge the intellect, download a copy ...." Laura Salkin, thinkspin.com

"Not very long, but a really good read. The author is intelligent, and points out some great inconsistencies in common thinking and action .... may have been channeling some George Carlin in a few areas." Briana Blair, Goodreads

" ... thought-provoking, and at times, hilarious. I particularly loved 'Bambi's cousin is going to tear you apart.' Definitely worth a read!" Nichole, Goodreads

"What she said!!! Pisses me off also! Funny, enjoyable and so right on!!!! Highly recommended." Vic, indigo.ca

Critical Thinking: An Appeal to Reason

"This book is worth its weight in gold." Daniel Millsap

"One of the books everyone should read. A lot of practical examples, clear and detailed sections, and tons of all kinds of logical fallacies analyzed under microscope that will give you a completely different way of looking to the everyday manipulations and will help you to avoid falling into the common traps. Highly recommended!" Alexander Antukh

"One of the best CT books I've read." G. Baruch, Goodreads

"This is an excellent critical thinking text written by a clever and creative critical thinker. Her anthology *What If* is excellent too: the short readings are perfect for engaging philosophical issues in and out of the classroom." Ernst Borgnorg

"Peg Tittle's *Critical Thinking* is a welcome addition to a crowded field. Her presentations of the material are engaging, often presented in a conversational discussion with the reader or student. The text's coverage of the material is wide-ranging. Newspaper items, snippets from *The Far Side*, personal anecdotes, emerging social and political debates, as well as LSAT sample questions are among the many tools Tittle employs to educate students on the elemental aspects of logic and critical thinking." Alexander E. Hooke, Professor of Philosophy, Stevenson University

What If?... Collected Thought Experiments in Philosophy

"Of all the collections of philosophical thought experiments I've read, this is by far the best. It is accessible, uses text from primary sources, and is very well edited. The final entry in the book— which I won't spoil for you—was an instant favorite of mine." Dominick Cancilla

"This is a really neat little book. It would be great to use in discussion-based philosophy courses, since the readings would be nice and short and to the point. This would probably work much better than the standard anthology of readings that are, for most students, incomprehensible." Nathan Nobis, Morehouse College

Should Parents be Licensed? Debating the Issues

"This book has some provocative articles and asks some very uncomfortable questions ...." Jasmine Guha, Amazon

"This book was a great collection of essays from several viewpoints on the topic and gave me a lot of profound over-the-(TV-)dinner-(tray-)table conversations with my husband." Lauren Cocilova, Goodreads

"You need a licence to drive a car, own a gun, or fish for trout. You don't need a licence to raise a child. But maybe you should ... [This book] contains about two dozen essays by various experts, including psychologists, lawyers and sociologists ...." Ian Gillespie, *London Free Press*

"... But the reformers are right. Completely. Ethically. I agree with Joseph Fletcher, who notes, "It is depressing ... to realize that most people are accidents," and with George Schedler, who states, "Society has a duty to ensure that infants are born free of avoidable defects. ... Traditionalists regard pregnancy and parenting as a natural right that should never be curtailed. But what's the result of this laissez-faire attitude? Catastrophic suffering. Millions of children born disadvantaged, crippled in childhood, destroyed in adolescence. Procreation cannot be classified as a self-indulgent privilege—it needs to be viewed as a life-and-death responsibility ...." Abhimanyu Singh Rajput, Social Tikka

Ethical Issues in Business: Inquiries, Cases, and Readings

"*Ethical Issues in Business* is clear and user-friendly yet still rigorous throughout. It offers excellent coverage of basic ethical theory, critical thinking, and many contemporary issues such as whistleblowing, corporate social responsibility, and climate change. Tittle's approach is not to tell students what to think but rather to get them to think—and to give them the tools to do so. This is the text I would pick for a business ethics course." Kent Peacock, University of Lethbridge

"This text breathes fresh air into the study of business ethics; Tittle's breezy, use-friendly style puts the lie to the impression that a business ethics text has to be boring." Paul Viminitz, University of Lethbridge

"A superb introduction to ethics in business." Steve Deery, *The Philosophers' Magazine*

"Peg Tittle wants to make business students think about ethics. So she has published an extraordinarily useful book that teaches people to question and analyze key concepts .... Take profit, for example .... She also analyzes whistleblowing, advertising, product safety, employee rights, discrimination, management and union matters, business and the environment, the medical business, and ethical investing ...." Ellen Roseman, *The Toronto Star*

more at
pegtittle.com

•

Writing as chris wind

This is what happens

"An interesting mix of a memoir and a philosophical work, together with some amazing poetry. ... *This is what happens* won't only be the book of the year for me, but it ranks high, top 5 on the best books ever read." Mesca Elin, mescalime.wordpress.com

"*This is what happens* relates how women are hamstrung by patriarchy ... the sexism both insidious and glaring that profoundly shaped Kris's life from its beginnings ... An incisive reflection on how social forces constrain women's lives. ... Great for fans of Sylvia Plath, Doris Lessing's *The Golden Notebook*." *Booklife*

Thus Saith Eve

"Short, but definitely entertaining ... and serious between the lines."
Lee Harmon, A Dubious Disciple Book Review

" ... a truly wonderful source of feminist fiction. In addition to being an extremely enjoyable and thought-provoking read, the monologues can also be used for audition and performance pieces." Katie M. Deaver, feminismandreligion.com

Snow White Gets Her Say

"Why isn't anyone doing this on stage? ... What a great night of theater that would be!" szferris, Librarything

"I loved the sassy voices in these stories, and the humor, even when making hard points." PJ O'Brien, Smashwords

Deare Sister

"You are clearly a writer of considerable talent, and your special ability to give expression to so many different characters, each in a uniquely appropriate style, makes your work fascinating and attractive. ... The pieces are often funny, sometimes sensitive, always creative. But they contain an enormous load of anger, and that is where I have problems. ... I know at least one feminist who would read your manuscript with delight (unfortunately she is not a publisher), who would roar with laughter in her sharing of your anger. ..." rejection letter from Black Moss Press

Particivision and other stories

"... your writing is very accomplished. ... *Particivision and other stories* is authentic, well-written, and certainly publishable ...." rejection letter from Turnstone Press

"... engaging and clever ...." rejection letter from Lester & Orpen Dennys, Publishers

"As the title indicates, this collection of stories is about getting into the thick of things, taking sides, taking action, and speaking out loud and clear, however unpopular your opinion may be. ... refreshingly out of the ordinary." Joan McGrath, *Canadian Book Review Annual*

dreaming of kaleidoscopes

"... a top pick of poetry and is very much worth considering. ..."
Midwest Book Review

Soliloquies: the lady doth indeed protest

"... not only dynamic, imaginative verse writing, but extremely intelligent and intuitive insight. ... I know many actresses who would love to get their hands on this material!" Joanne Zipay, Judith Shakespeare Company, NYC

"'Ophelia' is something of an oddity ... I found it curiously attractive."
Dinosaur

UnMythed

"... A welcome relief from the usual male emphasis in this area. There is anger and truth here, not to mention courage." Eric Folsom, *Next Exit*

"... With considerable skill and much care, chris wind has extrapolated truths from mythical scenarios and reordered them in modern terms. ... Wind handles these myths with and intellect. Her voice suggests that the relationship between the consciousness of the myth-makers and modern consciousness is closer than we would think." Linda Manning, *Quarry*

"Personally, I would not publish this stuff. This is not to say it isn't publishable—it's almost flawless stylistically, perfect form and content, etc., etc. It's perverse: satirical, biting, caustic, funny. Also cruel, beyond bitter, single-minded with a terminally limited point of view, and this individual may have read Edith Hamilton's Mythology but she/he certainly doesn't perceive the essential meanings of these myths. Or maybe does and deliberately twists the meaning to suit the poem. Likewise, in the etymological sense. Editorial revisions suggested? None, it's perfect. Market potential/readership targets: Everyone—this is actually marketable—you could sell fill Harbourfront reading this probably. General comments: You could actually make money on this stuff." anonymous reader report for a press that rejected the ms

Paintings and Sculptures

"You know that feeling—when you read the first page and you know you're going to like the book? That happened when I read the first poem. ... I loved 'Mona' and I could picture the scene; it might have happened that way, we'll never know ...." Mesca Elin, barnesandnoble.com

Satellites Out of Orbit

"*Satellites Out of Orbit* is an excellent and much recommended pick for unique fiction collections." Michael Dunford, *Midwest Book Review*

"... I also love the idea of telling the story from the woman's perspective, especially when the woman is only mentioned in passing in the official story, or not mentioned at all. ..." Shana, Tales of Minor Interest

"Our editorial board loved it. Our readers said it was the most feminist thing they've read in a long time." rejection letter from publisher

As I the Shards Examine / Not Such Stuff

"*Not Such Stuff* challenges us to rethink some of our responses to Shakespeare's plays and opens up new ways of experiencing them. ..." Jeff, secondat.blogspot.com

"This world premiere collection of monologs derive from eight female Shakespearian characters speaking from their hearts, describing aspects of their lives with a modern feminist sensibility. Deconstructing the traditional interpretations of some of the most fiercely fascinating female characters of all time, the playwright is able to "have at it" and the characters finally have their say. And oh, what tales they have to weave. ..." Debbie Jackson, dctheatrescene.com

Let Me Entertain You

"I found 'Let Me Entertain You' very powerful and visually theatrical." Ines Buchli

"I will never forget 'Let Me Entertain You.' It was brilliant." Kate Hurman

ProVocative

"Timely, thought-provoking, dark, and funny!" Kevin Holm-Hudson, WEFT

"... a great job making a point while being entertaining and interesting. ... Overall this is a fine work, and worth listening to." Kevin Slick, *gajoob*

The Art of Juxtaposition

"A cross between poetry, performance art, and gripping, theatrical sound collages. ... One of the most powerful pieces on the tape is 'Let Me Entertain You.' I sat stunned while listening to this composition." Myke Dyer, *Nerve*

"We found [this to be] unique, brilliant, and definitely not 'Canadian'. ... We were more than impressed with the material. *The Art of Juxtaposition* is filling one of the emptier spaces in the music world with creative and intelligent music-art." rejection letter from a record company

"Controversial feminist content. You will not be unmoved." Bret Hart, *Option*

"I've just had a disturbing experience: I listened to *The Art of Juxtaposition*. Now wait a minute; Canadian musicians are not supposed to be politically aware or delve into questions regarding sexual relationships, religion, and/or sex, racism, rape. They are supposed to write nice songs that people can tap their feet to and mindlessly inebriate themselves to. You expect me to play this on my show?" Travis B., CITR

"Wind mixes biting commentary, poignant insight and dark humor while unflinchingly tackling themes such as rape, marriage (as slavery), christianity, censorship, homosexuality, the state of native Americans, and other themes, leaving no doubt about her own strong convictions upon each of these subjects. Her technique is often one in which two or more sides to each theme are juxtaposed against one another (hence, the tape's title). This is much like her *Christmas Album* with a voice just as direct and pointed. Highly recommended." Bryan Baker, *gajoob*

"Thanks for *The Art of Juxtaposition* ... it really is quite a gem! Last Xmas season, after we aired 'Ave Maria' a listener stopped driving his car and phoned us from a pay phone to inquire and express delight." John Aho, CJAM

"Liked *The Art of Juxtaposition* a lot, especially the feminist critiques of the bible. I had calls from listeners both times I played 'Ave Maria.'" Bill Hsu, WEFT

"Every time I play *The Art of Juxtaposition* (several times by this point), someone calls to ask about it/you." Mars Bell, WCSB

"The work is stimulating, well-constructed, and politically apt with regard to sexual politics. (I was particularly impressed by 'I am Eve.')" Andreas Brecht Ua'Siaghail, CKCU

"We have found *The Art of Juxtaposition* to be quite imaginative and effective. When I first played it, I did not have time to listen to it before I had to be on air. When I aired it, I was transfixed by the power of it. When I had to go on mike afterward, I found I could hardly speak! To say the least, I found your work quite a refreshing change from all the fluff of commercial musicians who whine about lost love etc. Your work is intuitive, sensitive, and significant!" Erika Schengili, CFRC

"Interesting stuff here! Actually this has very little music, but it has sound bits and spoken work. Self-declared 'collage pieces of social commentary'. ...very thought-provoking and inspiring." *No Sanctuary*

more at
chriswind.net
and
chriswind.com

Also by Jass Richards

fiction

(the Rev and Dylan series)
The ReGender App
License to Do That
The Blasphemy Tour
The Road Trip Dialogues

(the Brett series)
Dogs Just Wanna Have Fun
This Will Not Look Good on My Resume

*A Philosopher, a Psychologist, and an Extraterrestrial
Walk into a Chocolate Bar*

TurboJetslams: Proof #29 of the Non-Existence of God

stageplays

Substitute Teacher from Hell

screenplays

Two Women, Road Trip, Extraterrestrial

performance pieces

Balls

nonfiction

Jane Smith's Translation Dictionary
Too Stupid to Visit

Writing as Peg Tittle

fiction

Fighting Words: notes for a future we won't have
Jess
Gender Fraud: a fiction
Impact
It Wasn't Enough
Exile
What Happened to Tom

screenplays

Exile
What Happened to Tom
Foreseeable
Aiding the Enemy
Bang Bang

stageplays

Impact
What Happened to Tom
Foreseeable
Aiding the Enemy
Bang Bang

audioplays

Impact

nonfiction

Just Think About It!
Sexist Shit that Pisses Me Off
No End to the Shit that Pisses Me Off
Still More Shit that Pisses Me Off
More Shit that Pisses Me Off
Shit that Pisses Me Off

Critical Thinking: An Appeal to Reason
What If? Collected Thought Experiments in Philosophy
Should Parents be Licensed? (editor)
Ethical Issues in Business: Inquiries, Cases, and Readings
Philosophy: Questions and Theories (contributing author)

Writing as chris wind

prose

This is what happens
Thus Saith Eve
Snow White Gets Her Say
Deare Sister
Particivision and other stories

poetry

dreaming of kaleidoscopes
Soliloquies: the lady doth indeed protest
UnMythed
Paintings and Sculptures

mixed genre

Satellites Out of Orbit
Excerpts

stageplays

As I the Shards Examine / Not Such Stuff
The Ladies' Auxiliary
Snow White Gets Her Say
The Dialogue
Amelia's Nocturne

performance pieces

I am Eve
Let Me Entertain You

audio work

ProVocative
The Art of Juxtaposition

CottageEscape.zyx

SATAN TAKES OVER

Jass Richards

Magenta

CottageEscape.zyx: Satan Takes Over
© 2023 Jass Richards

jassrichards.com

978-1-990083-03-7 (paperback)
978-1-990083-04-4 (epub)
978-1-990083-05-1 (pdf)

Published by Magenta

Magenta

Cover design by Jass Richards
Formatting and interior book design by Elizabeth Beeton

Library and Archives Canada Cataloguing in Publication

Title: CottageEscape.zyx : Satan takes over / Jass Richards.
Other titles: Cottage escape
Names: Richards, Jass, 1957- author.
Identifiers: Canadiana (print) 20220484406 | Canadiana (ebook) 20220484422 |
    ISBN 9781990083037 (softcover) | ISBN 9781990083044 (EPUB) | ISBN
    9781990083051 (PDF)
Classification: LCC PS8635.I268 C68 2023 | DDC C813/.6—dc23

At the time of publication, no one was using the domain of 'CottageEscape' dot *anything*, let alone dot '*zyx*' (which was not, at the time, a recognized domain extension); if, since then, it has become in use, note that nothing in this work of fiction is intended to be about *any actual* website.

Thanks to Jim Miller (a Grumpy Old Curmudgeon) and Jennifer Jilks (mymuskoka.blogspot.ca).

Those of you who have read *TurboJetslams: Proof #29 of the Non-Existence of God* might think that Vic lived happily ever after.

You'd be right about the happily.

You'd be wrong about the ever after.

What happened was the pandemic. At first, Vic thought that was a good thing. After all, everyone was told to 'Stay put' and 'Don't go out except for essentials'. But apparently, like the many men who thought 'No' meant 'Yes', a lot of people thought 'Stay put' meant 'Go somewhere'. Either that or a lot of people's definition of 'essentials' had an uncanny similarity to the definition of 'wants'.

So as soon as the pandemic hit, people from the city rushed to their cottages in the north to spread the virus. Like rats leaving a plague ship. In a caravan of SUVs.

People generously offered their weekends-and-summer-holidays cottage to all their relatives and friends, and their relatives' friends and their friends' relatives, and soon every cottage had continuous, and crowded, occupancy.

Those who lived in the rural north were concerned about the added strain on their already struggling services. Grocery stores, pharmacies, hospitals ... (The beer stores and the liquor stores didn't seem to experience any interruptions in supply or reduction in services. See above regarding 'essentials'.) Yes, the incomers promised to wear masks. And no, they wouldn't stop on the way, they'd bring what they needed with them, they wouldn't even have to go to the local grocery store.

Well, the last part was true. Because the local grocery store started offering order-and-deliver service: people from the city could call ahead, place their apocalypse order, and then cashiers would do their shopping for them while the rest of us waited at the check-outs, six feet apart, and then the baggers would deliver van loads of meat, eggs, milk, cheese, vegetables, fruit, hamburger buns, hot dog buns, ketchup, mustard, relish, steak sauce, salad dressing, marshmallows, cookies, chips, chocolate bars, frozen pizza, ice cream, toothpaste, soap, shampoo, and toilet paper—lots of toilet paper—to their cottages. While the rest of us waited at the check-outs. Six feet apart. Of course, the local grocery store charged a hefty fee for the service, but people who had two homes either had a hefty income or a hefty debt such that an extra couple hundred here and there wouldn't make much difference. In fact, the sooner they could declare bankruptcy, the sooner the rest of us would, one way or another, pay their debts for them.

And then, when there seemed to be no end in sight—because when the geneticists got to the omega variant, they could just go back and use all the letters of the alphabet they missed—the rentals appeared.

Vic had thought that what with people losing their jobs or getting fewer shifts, the non-stop construction and renovation— with its ever-present noise of chain saws, excavation machinery, circular saws, nail guns, power drills ... would stop. Or at least diminish.

She was wrong. Very wrong.

Opportunistic wannabe-entrepreneurs stepped forward in droves (well, raced to the bank in droves) (the opportunistic banks) to provide five-star accommodations for the rats. Within a year, there were 5 brand new houses on Paradise Lake, all built specifically to be rental properties. That means the houses had a living room with leather couches, a huge flat-screen tv, and a small bar, an entertainment center with its own huge flat-screen tv and a playroom corner, a kitchen with marble counters and stainless steel appliances, two full bathrooms, three bedrooms, *and* a couple bunkies, so they could say 'sleeps twelve' and charge $7,000 a week for a multi-family rental. Such rental properties also had a beach with a firepit, a yard with a swing set, and two docks—one for the kayaks and canoes (provided), one for the jetslams and motorboats (bring your own).

And there were more to come. In fact, there was such a frenzy of development (think 'goldrush'), it was hard to find a contractor, so one guy started the excavation himself on his newly-bought waterfront property. Which was, essentially, a slice of cliff. The inspector took one look at the excavator half in the lake and stamped "FAIL" on his report.

Picturesque (ugly) cottage signs sprouted up along the roadside almost overnight. *Our Summer Home, TGIF, The Family Cottage* ... (Alongside signs for a quarry, a logging company, the hardware store, a construction company, and the beer store. There were no signs for a fabric and yarn store, or a bakery, or dance lessons at the rec center. The Township stank of male armpit.)

Vic hated the signs. They were like pus-filled boils on the otherwise beautiful forest that edged both sides of the roads. Some signs had the name of the rental property faux-carved onto a faux-paddle. (No doubt for the properties featuring a fleet of jetslams.) Others showed smiling beaver and bear, reminiscent of Disney fairy tales. Still others were— Well, they were *all* advertising. No one who actually *lived* on Paradise Lake posted a sign indicating that they lived there. Why would they? Because there were road signs (Spruce Lane, Sunset Lane, and Paradise Lake Lane) and house numbers. If you wanted to tell someone where you lived, you just gave your address: 13 Sunset Lane (or whatever). (And if people couldn't *read* the road signs, well, how were they going to read the cottage signs?) There was simply no need for the signs. At every intersection.

Except *as* advertising. And what they were advertising was a lie: it was 'cottage kitsch' meets 'myth of the north'. The signs fostered the delusion that people were entering the remote wilderness 'up north' (so empty, the roads had no names), where, because it was so uninhabited (evidence to the contrary right next door) (not to mention all the *other* cottage signs), they could do whatever they wanted.

If they thought instead that they were just leaving their own neighbourhood and renting a house in the middle of someone else's neighbourhood (and would have to act accordingly), the whole endeavour would lose its charm. And the $7,000/week price tag.

One time, some strangers stopped Vic on the lane, on her way to her mailbox, and asked her why she was so rude. Apparently they'd waved at her when she'd kayaked past the cottage they were renting and she hadn't waved back. WTF? She was supposed to wave at people she didn't know? And she'd been paddling at the time! She was supposed to stop, and put her paddle down, just to return their wave? She could have nodded, she supposed, but really, she just wasn't into that. (She'd bought her cabin-on-a-lake-in-the-forest for the solitude and the beauty. Sigh.) And she suspected they weren't either. When they walked through *their* neighbourhood, back home, should they ever do that, did they wave, nod, and/or smile at everyone they saw, strangers included? No, it was part of the whole 'We're at the cottage having a fun time with all these nice people' thing. A sort of tourist delusion. Vic wanted to shout at them—and she might, next time—that she wasn't part of their 'cottage experience'. This wasn't *The Truman Show*. She was a real person. She did not come into existence when they arrived and disappear when they left. She *lived* there, *24/7*, in a house that was just up the road from the house they were renting.

The cottagers who had not yet offered their cottage to family and friends when they weren't using it soon started doing so, suggesting a modest financial contribution to the increasing property taxes triggered by the increasing property prices triggered by the increasing number of rental properties (and the bidding wars instigated by greedy real estate agents).

There was no change in what could be called unofficial and therefore unregulated trailer parks—lots upon which a trailer was parked, understood to be the prelude to the construction of at least a cottage (within two years, according to Township law) (though 'two' seemed to mean 'eventually') (or 'never'—because taxes for a trailer were a mere $200 compared to well over ten times that for a cottage). No change except that where previously, it was not unusual for there to be 3 trailers, 2 of which were in various states of collapse (it was cheaper to just leave them there than have them towed to a scrap yard), now it was not unusual to see 7 trailers, 3 of which were in various states of collapse. Because like the cottagers, the trailer park owners were inviting their family and friends ...

So. Do the math.

No wait, I'll do it for you.

In the beginning, when Vic first bought her cabin on Paradise Lake, three hours north of Toronto, a good half hour off the main highway, there were 10 houses on the lake: 5 were occupied by permanent residents and 5 were summer cottages. Slowly, over the course of twenty years, both doubled—surprising Vic because she'd thought that all that forest was Crown land—making 20 houses: 10 permanent residences and 10 summer cottages. That meant 20 people at the lake year-round (say 2 people per permanent residence, times 10) and another 30 (2 people per cottage, times 10, plus kids) on the weekends and during their two weeks of summer holiday, but since those 30 would never be up at the same time, let's say year-round occupancy was 20, summer occupancy was another 20, so 40, max.

Now, there were 30 houses (that's 3 times as many): in addition to the initial 5 new houses, another 5 were built on what *had been* Crown land—Vic was dismayed to discover that the Ministry could, and apparently did, sell Crown land for cottage lots when the relevant municipality claimed said sales would contribute to its "economic development objectives". (Since the additional tax revenue would surely be offset by the additional road expense, the enthusiasm with which the municipality filed such claims with the Ministry gave one the impression that the council members thought the additional tax money would go directly into their own pockets.)

Due to various sales (in one case, the owners wanted to be closer to kids, grandkids, and hospitals; in all of the other cases, the owners fled in disappointment, despair, and disgust) and subsequent transformations, only 7 of the now 30 were permanent residences, only 6 were traditional summer cottages (arguably: 2 were trophy houses, cottages purchased then renovated, merely for inviting colleagues for the weekends and showing off), 2 were multi-family conglomerate summer cottages, and 15 were rental properties. And there were now 4 trailer parks.

That meant there were 14 people living at the lake year-round (the 7 permanent residences, times 2 per), but during the summer (and spring and fall and sometimes winter, because the rentals would try to maximize their occupancy/income), there were an additional 24 (the traditional 6 cottages, times, let's say, 4 per—only a few had kids, but they all had family and friends who would come up when they weren't there), plus 16 (the 2 multi-family conglomerates, times, let's say, 8 per—two families at a time seemed to be the norm), plus 150 (the 15 rentals, times, let's say, 10 per), plus 64 (the 4 trailer parks, times 4 can-be-occupied trailers, times 4 occupants per). For a total of 268. Compared to the pre-pandemic summer occupancy of 40. That's—I said I'd do the math for you—ALMOST SEVEN TIMES AS MANY PEOPLE. At the lake. Pretty much on any given day from May to October.

And compared to the people-who-actually-live-there occupancy? There were, let's see, 268 vs. 14—**ALMOST TWENTY TIMES AS MANY PEOPLE**. At the lake. Pretty much on any given day from May to October. People who could talk, and walk, and, more to the point, who could drive jetslams and ATVs and—

You can see why Vic bought a gun.

Ha-ha. Just kidding.

She didn't have to.

Shiggles was no more and her new little sweetheart, Shoogles, was far more vocal. Vic had only some success teaching her to 'just watch' when she raced to the gate or to the dock to shout something at passersby. Which, honestly, was just fine. Given Vic's desire to also shout something at passersby ...

But it occurred to her, a little more vulnerable now due to age, that she should do the same. Just watch.

So she started keeping her small camera beside her when she sat down at the water. (And bought a second one to keep in her kayak.) It had a powerful zoom lens. After all, she had, whether she wanted it or not, a front row seat: a new vintage lounge chair with repaired webbing and a comfy cushion, sitting so very nicely on her new extra-wide dock. The old vintage lounge chair had, one day, decided quite suddenly and without warning to stop being a chair: all the UV-weakened webbing tore at once, and she found herself ass-hard on the dock in the middle of a jigsaw puzzle of aluminum frame pieces. The old dock, on the other hand, had, one day, let out a big sigh then just slowly leaned, a little, then a little more, eventually settling ever so gently on the bottom of the lake at a perfect 45 degree angle. (She had appreciated the warning. And the slowness with which she was lowered into the cold water.) So. A front row seat. At her own entertainment center.

She quickly discovered the power of the camera. Perhaps people thought she was actually taking pictures and videos. (She was.) Perhaps people feared she would post them online. (She did.) With appropriate captions. (Of course.) "Moron renter pretends he's not trespassing" (some guy standing on the shoreline next to someone's dock, fishing). "Family of four can't tell a private beach from a public beach" (said family of four having a picnic on the Campbell's picnic table and using the float toys they kept in a bin beside their kayak).

O ne day some kid drove his jetslam straight into a ten-by-ten raft that had been floating freely in the middle of the lake. Those who lived at Paradise Lake knew it was out there, somewhere. It had been making the rounds for a good two weeks, often getting stuck (safely, though unaesthetically) in a patch of shoreline muck, then when the wind changed and rose to strength (or when someone gave it a few hard jabs with a kayak paddle), it would become free and resume floating, to somewhere else (out of sight).

The raft had 'PROPERTY OF THE ROBSONS' in huge red letters on its side. So you'd think the kid—it was the Robson's grandkid (one of the many grandkids) (of the many Robsons, the ones who had the Robson cottage for the first week of July every year)—would've veered away at the last moment to avoid hitting it. But maybe he couldn't read. Or didn't know his last name. After all, he was only six years old.

B ut, as Shoogles would attest, the whole 'just watch' thing was only so much fun.

Satan Takes Over

So Vic bought a megaphone. It had three voice distortion settings: Darth Vader, Jack Nicholson, and Alvin the Chipmunk. For good measure, she planned to aim it across the cove when she used it, figuring that the natural echo chamber that had nearly driven her insane (before she started wearing earplugs as a matter of routine) would confuse people as to the source. Or they'd assume it was the Taylors—whose shit was still sitting there on the peninsula across the cove, in her face all day long. (Or would be if she hadn't hung strips of gorgeous Dupioni silk across the middle of every lakeside window in her cabin: fiery orange in one, shimmering fuchsia in another, and iridescent gold in the third.) (As for when she was down at the water, she'd attached branches to her dock, vertically, every two feet, from the middle of the front along all of the right side, and then strung some equally gorgeous Ashland maple leaf garlands from branch to branch, at just the right height. Sitting in her chair, positioned just so, the entire shoreline was hidden. She saw only water and then trees and sky. Not one dock, not one cottage, not one light at night ... and, best of all, none of the Taylor's shit. It was amazing, the power of 'out of sight out of mind' ...)

She had occasion to use her brand new shiny megaphone the very next day. Shortly after she settled down at the water, a fishing boat puttered into the cove and parked a mere ten feet from her dock. (Good thing their over-priced on-board fish-finding tech didn't indicate that the fish they were trying to catch was *under* her dock.)

And then one of the guys stood and began to urinate over the side of the boat. She reached for her megaphone, set it to Darth Vader, and called out "Hey, stop that! The lake is not a toilet!"

In his rush to zip up and turn to look (because of course he hadn't seen her sitting there, just ten feet away), or maybe lacking the coordination to do both at the same time, perhaps especially since he was probably pissing pure beer, he fell overboard.

His buddies didn't notice.

The guy drowned.

Oh well.

She continued to put the megaphone to good use throughout the summer whenever she heard a conversation (two-sided if there were two people in the boat; one-sided if there was one person with a cellphone in the boat). Which was whenever a boat was parked ... well, anywhere. Because, Vic wanted to explain, when you're in the middle of the small generally-calm lake (or anywhere on the water, actually) and you're talking to a friend, you may as well be talking *to everyone who's there and outside at the time*. Seriously. That's how well sound travels across water. Haven't you noticed? No, you've been too busy talking.

Instead, she'd picked up her megaphone. Set it to Alvin.

"La la la la la la." She would have put her hands over her ears if she thought they could see her. But she was hiding behind the trees.

The conversation stopped.

Then resumed.

"La la la la la la la la."

The conversation stopped.

Then resumed.

"La la la la la la la la."

Satan Takes Over

The claim that 'Insanity is doing the same thing over and over and expecting different results' did occur to her.

Turned out it wasn't who was the more sane that mattered, but who had the greater capacity to persist.

Vic had already been taking a mask with a charcoal filter with her when she went kayaking, for when jetslams and motorboats insisted on passing her and farting their gasoline fumes in her face. Little fishing boats were especially annoying because there was always a man at the helm, a man who simply *had* to pass her—not only was she *paddling*, but she was a *woman*—but then because the man was fishing, he'd slow to a crawl just a few feet in front of her. No amount of obvious coughing and putting her hand over her mouth made a dent in the cement of the guy's brain.

When she screamed 'Thanks for the headache', the man would smile. A woman was paying attention to him. How studly was he!?

When she gave him a lecture regarding the effects on brain chemistry of two-stroke engine exhaust, explaining that if you can smell it, you've already ingested a huge dose of benzene, formaldehyde, and polycyclic aromatic hydrocarbons, he'd smile. A woman was *talking* to him. How studly was he!?

Now she took a second mask with her, a pandemic mask. She'd put it on when she and Shoogles got out to walk, which they did at the airport road (yes, there was an airport on the river, and while it wasn't used very often, when it was, everyone on the lake knew it) and at the park, since it was now likely there would be so many more people at both locations. (That is to say, since it was now likely there would be *someone* at both locations.)

At first, she didn't understand why so many people were offended when she put it on, then—ah. They were so self-centered, the idea of altruism was completely foreign to them: it didn't even *occur* to them that she was wearing a mask to protect *them* against possible infection (should she be infectious but asymptomatic). Which, honestly, made her consider *not* wearing a pandemic mask ...

She even started wearing it when she walked to the end of the lane to get her mail, because she'd often meet renters wandering around, looking for a Starbuck's, probably ...

"Your mask makes me uncomfortable," one woman said to her one day. Having come within six feet of Vic to do so.

"Yeah? Well your presence makes me uncomfortable."

Actually, what Vic said instead was, "I'm infected. But I'll take it off if you like," she added, raising her hands to her face.

But the woman had already fled.

Cool.

On days too windy to go kayaking, she headed into the forest. Sadly, it had been logged (yes, with 32 million hectares of Crown forest in the province, they had to log a section close to a residential area), but new growth was finally starting to hide the mess that had been left, and after a mile, she was in deep forest again. One day on her way in, she noticed a piece of litter (she no longer picked up the garbage twice a year like she used to, there was simply too much; well, that and the last time she'd done it, some guy in a pick-up truck had slowed down to insult her), a sheet of paper that had 'The Paradise Lake Property Owners Association' across the top. Hm. She hadn't known any of her neighbours could read. Let alone write. She certainly hadn't known of any such association. She'd actually thought of forming a residents' association, long ago, but as a woman, she had what she called the Reverse Midas touch: anything *she* suggested was considered stupid and not worth anyone's attention. She'd have to wait until a man came up with the same idea, and, well, that just never happened.

Then it registered that it was an *property* owners' association, not a *residents'* association. Hm. Probably spearheaded by the owner of one of the 'sleeps twelve' rentals. No matter. She was a property owner *and* a resident. So she went to the next meeting, time and place conveniently, but barely, legible on the many-times-run-over piece of paper.

"Hello," one of the men—she saw immediately that everyone present was male—said from his position at the head of the table. They'd rented the small room at the Legion. "You are representing ... ?"

It was such an odd question, it threw her for a second.

Ah. They were asking who her husband was. Because NO GIRLS ALLOWED.

"Myself." She took several steps into the room.

They stared at her.

Finally, one of the other men spoke. "This is a property owners' association."

"Yeah," she said. Then realized that she had to educate them. Sigh. "Women have been allowed to own property since 1884. This is 2022," she added. Just in case.

"Your name?" The head guy tapped his laptop.

"Vic Jensen."

He scrolled down, reading.

"You're not on the list."

"What list?"

"The list of property owners."

"You have a list?" Wait a minute. A while ago, when she wanted permission to cross an as-yet-undeveloped piece of property in order to get to a trail on Crown land (to go for a walk with Shoogles at the halfway point on their six-hour round trip paddle), she'd gone to the Township to ask for the owner's name and phone number; they refused to tell her, because, they said, the Freedom of Information Act prohibited them from doing so. (The complete name was The Freedom of Information and *Protection of Privacy* Act.)

"Where did you get that list?" she asked as she walked to the head of the table to take a look. He closed his laptop. Of course. Don't let the women know—anything.

"We put it together."

"Well then."

Silence.

And another sigh. "You obviously didn't do a good job. It's incomplete."

"Could we see a copy of your deed?"

Yes, of course, I have it right here with me. She sighed yet again. Women have to *prove* their credentials. Men are just *assumed* to *have* credentials. Whatever credentials they *say* they have.

"She must be a new owner," another one of the men said to the head guy. As if Vic wasn't there. Because women are invisible.

"When did you buy your property?" the head guy asked.

"1988," she replied. "So I'm *not* a new owner," she said to the other guy. "In fact, I'm the oldest owner on the lake." She meant she was the one who'd owned property the longest, but when she looked around the room—well, hell. "I've owned property here since before some of you were even born." (How did a thirty-something come to have enough money for not just one house, but two? *And* be able to support not only himself but, let's say, three other people?)

"Ah. Our list goes back only to 2020."

Right. When the rentals started showing up.

"So, what, before you all arrived, *when* you all arrived, you didn't think anyone was already living here?" She looked around at the blank faces. "Does the name 'Christopher Columbus' ring a bell?"

"Who?" the head guy consulted his list.

Another sigh.

"Is Janet Taylor on your list?"

He looked again at his list. "No."

"Ellen Campbell?"

After another quick moment, he shook his head.

"Deb Dresher?" She assumed, hoped, the deeds were in the wives' names too ...

After three more names, she left. Figured she'd given them some food for thought.

But all they did was change their name. They became the Paradise Lake Rental Property Owners Association.

So, denied input through the 'official' channel, once again (see 'The History of Women'), Vic went online. There were many portals for cottage rentals, all of them listing hundreds of rentals, most of which promised some sort of high-quality escape. She found the webpage for every rental on Paradise Lake. (The pages made for interesting, and entertaining, reading: most of the time she didn't even recognize Paradise Lake, and given the logical necessity of non-contradiction, it was clear that they couldn't all be describing the same place.) Then she set up a new email address. Ten, in fact. All of them with a male name. Because. She googled a bit, downloaded some VPN software, then set up a connection. And then she registered at all of the cottage rental portal sites, bookmarking for easy access the pages advertising rentals on Paradise Lake. Only actual renters could post feedback, but most portals had a 'Contact the owner' option, and for those that didn't, if she filled in the rental inquiry form, she could attach a message to the owner. Sometimes she'd say she was a permanent resident, but when she wanted more protection, because of Shoogles, she'd say she was a weekender. Or the friend of a weekender. Or renting nearby.

She had occasion to use one of her email aliases almost immediately.

Satan Takes Over

Every time Vic went kayaking, she paddled up the creek that branched off, or into, the lake, just past the houses. It was the prettiest, quietest, part of her paddle: Crown land on both sides and too shallow for a motor. (Though the asshole with the quad-jetslam tried it every year. In case, what, someone had dredged it since the previous summer? Idiot.) Pity it was only a few hundred metres before the near-impassable rapids. She had, a couple times, made the long and difficult walk up the rapids, tugging her kayak behind her and falling repeatedly on the slimy rocks, but, surprisingly, what was on the other side wasn't nearly as pretty, so instead she just sat for a while in her kayak at the rapids, listening to the wonderful rush of the tumbling water and hoping to see a deer or a moose (she'd seen both on occasion, as well as a fawn and a pair of mooselets). Or she got out and went for a walk with Shoogles on the path along the creek back toward the last house (previously Sarah's house, now *Serenity*) at the point of entry.

One day when she got out to do so, she was appalled to see that someone had set up a campfire spot. Right there. In the forest. In the prettiest, quietest, part of … Since there were some split log benches on stumps arranged around a flat rock circle (there was no firepit per se—they'd brought a chain saw with them but not a shovel?), and a small pile of wood nearby, it was clear they intended to return and have another campfire. And another.

She picked out four scorched cans from the charred bits of wood, grabbed an old tin box they'd hung on a tree branch, then left.

It was Sarah who had cleared the path, but Vic wasn't sure where her property ended and Crown land began. So she covered both bases.

First, she sent a message to the owner of *Serenity* (who, she'd noticed when she'd read his rental webpage, promoted "a calming path through the woods"):

I was alarmed to come across a campfire spot complete with benches in the bush about a quarter mile from your house. I'm assuming you put it there. (If I'm wrong, my apologies, and please disregard this note.) (Actually, no, don't disregard this note: your house is at risk.)

Short version:
What the hell were you thinking?

Long version:

1. The ground there is covered with dry tinder: leaves and conifer needles.
2. Hanging overhead are dead, dry branches.
3. The wood I saw piled nearby is too long to fit in the rock circle.
4. It's also the kind of wood that'll spark like crazy.
5. I didn't see a pail of water near at hand.
6. The spot is not at all accessible by road, so if a fire ever gets out of hand, fire trucks won't be able to deal with it until it reaches the road. On which several people live.

You might be responsible about having an outdoor fire, even checking every day to see whether there's a fire ban (sure to increase in frequency as our summers get hotter and drier), but you might rent (unknowingly) to a bunch of yahoos who get drunk or stoned and then go traipsing into the forest to commune with the wood-sprites and next thing we know, the entire neighbour-hood will be up in flames.

Then, she sent a letter to the Ministry of Natural Resources:

I read on the MNR website that it's permissible for anyone to start a fire anywhere on Crown land at any time. ARE Y'ALL FUCKING CRAZY?

[Attached: images of the forest fires that raged through the northwest part of the province in 2018]

Later in the day, she remembered the scorched cans she'd forgotten to unload. And the tin. Curious, she opened it. And found a little note:

"The Explorer Series"
GeoCache #47

Steve Bennet
Don Poulson
Mike McGinn
Darryl Nesmith

Congratulations, you found it!
Please do not disturb.
This is an official game piece.

www.geocaching.com

What the hell? She went online. And discovered that geo-caching was an organized continent-wide scavenger hunt. People all over the place were hiding shit. All over the place. *What the hell!* There were rules to follow, but still.

As soon as she finished reading through the various pages, she used the contact form:

> I'd like to report a geocache "found in an unsuit-able location": four of your members have cut down trees on Crown land (illegal) and created a campfire spot where the risk of fire is very high (idiotic) and very close to many people's homes (inconsiderate). Furthermore, the presence of park-like benches in natural forest surely qualifies as "defacing" public property.
>
> They left a note: "Please do not disturb." Excuse me? YOU, you little fuckers, PLEASE DO NOT DISTURB! This is beautiful forest. Leave it the fuck alone.
>
> The note also said "This is an official game piece." Again, excuse me? FUCKING MEN! You think your insatiable need to compete gives you the right to do whatever you want wherever you want whenever you want. You think SPORT and THE GAME trumps everything and everyone. I can't go into the forest AT ALL during hunting season because YOU MUST BE ALLOWED to engage in your 'sport' of killing harmless animals. So, you know what you can do with your OFFICIAL GAME PIECE?

A week later, when Vic rounded the first bend in the little creek, she saw smoke. And started paddling furiously. When she arrived ...

A bucket brigade without buckets is like a sad game of telephone: by the time the water reaches the last person, it isn't really water, it's air. They were passing air from cupped hands to cupped hands. Unsurprisingly, it did nothing to put out the spreading flames.

She tossed one of the fire extinguishers she'd tucked behind her seat to one of the guys who was just standing there. It hit him in the head. He fell down.

One of his three friends picked it up and tossed it back to her, smiling.

Shoogles, perched on the prow, ducked. (Then quickly scooted *under* the prow.)

Vic jammed her kayak between some fallen trees and the shore on the other side of the creek, no time to secure it, and told Shoogles—probably unnecessarily—to STAY!

Then she waded over with the other fire extinguisher. (Who carries two fire extinguishers in her kayak?) She clambered up the steep incline and— She saw that they'd thrown their cellphones onto the fire, probably after realizing they didn't have any buckets of water to throw onto it, perhaps, or perhaps not, also after realizing there was no cell reception along the creek.

She'd never used a fire extinguisher before and relieved to discover there was enough foam, though barely, to make half a circle around the spreading fire.

She went back into the creek and retrieved the other fire extinguisher from the shallows. Would it still work? One would hope. Yes. Good. She finished the circle she hoped would enclose the spreading fire. And it might, she thought, as long as there was no snap, crackle, pop.

Then she waded back to her kayak, emptied one of her waterproof bags, trudged back across and handed it to one of the standing guys. Not the one who'd kindly tossed her fire extinguisher back to her.

He put it on his head. And grinned at her.

She waded back to her kayak yet again, emptied her other waterproof bag, made her way back across the creek and started using it as a pail.

"Water balloons!" The guys giggled.

Once all of the flames were extinguished, she used a long branch to poke at the mess, dousing every still glowing ember that she uncovered.

Finally, satisfied, she took a picture of the foursome—one still out and on the ground, another still be-hatted, all four grinning like idiots.

She heaved the only backpack she saw into the deepest part of the creek, then went to their parked canoes, grabbed their paddles, and jettisoned every one of them up the rapids, surpassing by far the women's world records for both shotput and javelin, respectively. (Including the one set by that 325 pound six-foot tall guy who suddenly felt like a woman and so was allowed to enter the women's events—no, wait, that was weightlifting—doesn't matter—even though he hadn't yet bothered to take estrogen, let alone to get his dick turned inside out to make a vagina.) (Vic suspected the women whose records he'd broken would take care of that.)

Finally, she spoke. "Who's got the matches?"

They all patted their pockets. Except the guy on the ground. The fourth guy pulled out a box of matches, some rolling papers, and a little baggie.

"I do!" he said happily.

"Thanks." She pocketed all of it.

She then set both canoes adrift, before returning to Shoogles and her kayak.

"Good dog!" she told her, because she was—she'd watched anxiously from the cockpit the whole time, not once even *thinking* about getting out to help—then paddled off, escorting the two canoes into open water.

When the owner of *Serenity* received (from a 'Dave Suzuki') the photograph she'd taken of the foursome, along with the one she'd taken of their proud note in the little tin, he put it all together, correctly, and sued the four men, the geocache organization, and the MNR. For reckless endangerment and negligent behaviour.

Encouraged by that success, she considered using another one of her alias emails for another situation.

By way of context, back when Vic and Shiggles were walking on the trail through the forest, they discovered that some guy had set traps near the trail. She'd met his pick-up coming out of the forest and saw two dead wolves in the cargo bed. That first time, she was ... silent. Remembering the gorgeous cream-and-tan young wolf she'd caught by surprise when she'd rounded a corner one bright, summer day. (It had been just as surprised, trotting along with such oh-what-a-beautiful-day in its gait. They'd stared at each for a long, amazing, moment, and then it turned and went back the way it had come.)

Not leg hold traps, snare traps. So she went online and learned how to loosen them (there's a little metal clothespin clip that when squeezed, lets you feed the wire back through, making the loop bigger, thus loosening it when it's strangling someone's neck, and enabling you, eventually, to slip it off). Then she taught Shiggles to avoid them (they approached one, and when Shiggles walked toward it, she screamed 'LEAVE IT!!' so loud Shiggles cowered at her feet—perfect).

A while later, when they were walking with one of Shiggles' friends, Vic suddenly realized Bingo wasn't with them anymore. Then she realized where they were. SHIT! Shiggles already knew to stay on the main path at that point, but— 'STAY!!' she yelled loudly with as much authority as she could muster, then went off-path looking for Bingo, stumbling about, nose-blind, unable to track the scent of the bait as Bingo probably had ... He was good. So good. He'd stayed. When she found him five minutes later, he was quivering but otherwise absolutely still, the wire around his neck, tight but not choking him. She felt for the clothespin, pinched it, then fed the wire back through until she could lift the loop off his head.

Whiskey, as awkward as he was enthusiastic, had gotten his leg caught but in full random gallop, had pulled the snare stake right out of the ground. Then, frantic at the thing clinging to his leg, galloped even more randomly. She was able to stop him—it helped that he tackled her—and got the damn thing off. No physical damage.

(Juno hadn't been so lucky. It had been twenty hours before his owner had found him. He'd survived, but had a permanent scar around his neck. And refused to leave the yard ever again.)

The second time she met his pick-up moving slowly along the trail, she stopped him and asked if he'd mark where he set his traps. Maybe just tie a ribbon on a tree at the trail's edge. Apparently that was too much trouble.

So she contacted the Township, but they said they had no jurisdiction over Crown land.

So she called the Ministry. Was that legal? Yes. To put traps so close to where people, and dogs (and kids, she added as an afterthought), went for a walk? Yes. Can you not require the traps to be a good distance from the path, maybe a hundred metres or so? As soon as the words were out of her mouth, she understood. Fat ass in a pick-up. No way he could carry, or even drag, eighty pounds of dead wolf more than a hundred *feet* through what she liked to call 'Canadian jungle'—a dense tangle of undergrowth and fallen trees. (She'd once covered *two* hundred feet, chasing after Shoogles who was chasing after a rabbit—in case she got stuck—Shoogles, not the rabbit—because it was winter and the snow was thigh deep—and it was the best, or worst, work-out of her life.) (And she used to *run* on *snowshoes,* training for marathons.) And in winter, well, his snowmobile was sure to get stuck in the first ten feet.

Everyone had a right to use Crown land, she was told. She was *so* sick of that response. Because people didn't have an *absolute* right—to *anything.* There were rules about what you could and could not do. And the Ministry guy knew it. You couldn't cut down trees on Crown land. That would be theft. (But you can cut down wolves. In the prime of their lives.)

Can you at least require that trap locations be marked, so people know?

Well, the guy probably sets his traps in the same place every year, the man replied.

Right. Okay. So eventually, by tracking his pick-up tires after rain and snow, she found three locations. And half a dozen snare traps at each. She unstrung every one of them.

Next time she checked, they'd been reset.

She undid his work again.

He never did get the message.

So when Vic noticed that several of the rentals allowed dogs, and *Rover's Retreat* actually promoted its pet-friendly status, she (well, a 'Pete Singer') sent messages to all of them, describing the situation. Generally, with respect to ... intervention, she'd intended to wait until something actually happened, because she figured that would increase the likelihood of something actually changing, but in this case, the something would happen to a *dog*.

Reportedly, when the owner of *Rover's Retreat* called the Ministry, he was told, 'Sure, no problem, he'd call the guy right away and tell him to move his traps, and he'd make a note for a province-wide amendment, he hadn't known traps were being set so close to the trail.'

Hadn't known, my ass. Thought Vic.

(Had the owner threatened to sue? Or had he just been male at the time of the call?)

Regardless, lo and behold, no more traps could be set within 100 metres of any path that was used by people, on foot. Which pretty much stopped trapping because, as Vic had figured, no one in the Township who was into killing animals was strong enough to retrieve their distant kills on foot without suffering a heart attack. Which is exactly what happened to what's-his-name.

S ometimes, however, her intervention was more—'old-school' ...

The lake was connected to its river in a misaligned way at a pretty little cove with seven houses, one of which was now a rental property and one of which was a multi-family cottage with a driveway that seemed perpetually crammed with RVs and pick-ups with double-wide trailers.

Typically, when Vic was paddling up the lake, she hugged the shoreline to be safe, rounded the point enough for the jetslams at *Weekend Getaway* and the multi-family cottage to see her, then like a child crossing a busy street with no crosswalk (let alone a crossing guard), she'd paddle as quickly as she could across the cove in the straight line marking the shortest distance from the shore on the one side to the marsh on the other, at which point she could continue safely, and leisurely, up the river. She suspected other kayakers, and there were a few now, did the same.

One day, right in the middle of that straight line, there was a pile of rocks. What the hell? It was a good fifty feet out. At first, she thought one of the jetslammers had put it there, hoping—what? That she'd paddle full-steam into it? And then stop paddling on the lake altogether?

Then she thought it was one of those 'I was here' markers she'd started seeing on hiking trails. (They annoyed her to no end. Must humans contaminate every square inch of the planet with their presence?)

She started dismantling the pile of rocks. (Shoogles wisely got off the prow and into the cockpit.)

Suddenly a jetslam roared toward her. Only the pile of rocks prevented him from slamming right into her.

"What the fuck are you doing?" He stood up, straddling his seat. Be big.

"Knocking over this pile of rocks." She pushed another rock off the pile into the water.

"Are you crazy?"

What?

"Look," she said, "if you want to put up some stupid 'I was here' marker, do it on your own property. This isn't even *close* to your property. You don't own the lake." She pushed another rock off the pile.

"You fucking bitch!" He zoomed in an angry circle around her.

Despite the resulting waves, she easily managed to push yet another rock off the pile.

"There's a sandbar here!" he screamed. "It's a marker for my renters to avoid it!"

She looked to the mess of jetslams on the beach. Then she looked across the water. "Why don't you just tell them to aim for that dead tree?" she nodded. Then added, "No need for a pile of rocks right in the middle of the kayaking path." Another rock tumbled off the pile.

He zoomed in another circle around her, enraged. "It took me *two hours* to build that!"

"And it took me two minutes to destroy." She grinned at him.

Well, that did it. (How to make a man totally lose his shit: Challenge him. While female. Say 'No.' Or just knock over his pile of rocks.) He zoomed up a furious foam, shouting and gesticulating. Fortunately, he couldn't disembark—well, he could, but then he'd look *really* foolish—and at close quarters, she had the more agile watercraft. (Jetslams had no 'reverse'.)

Even so, he'd thrown *such* a tantrum, she decided, when she saw the pile rocks back in place next time she paddled, to just leave it. After all, he could figure out where she lived.

Come winter, the pile would get covered with snow and look like a snow drift. The snowmobilers racing up the lake wouldn't be able to resist it. She wondered how many fatalities there'd be before someone thought to post a warning sign. (Eight.)

And after each one, she sent an anonymous note to the family conveying her sympathy—yes she could do that; she just had to concentrate really hard—and the name of the guy who'd put pile of rocks there. (Which would be needed for a wrongful death suit.)

And sometimes, no intervention on her part was needed ...

By way of context, whenever she and Shiggles had gone kayaking, she'd let Shiggles out at the stretch past the airport to splish splash along the shore or run the path a few feet in, eventually coming to Harley's cabin, at which there were often geese to chase with great enthusiasm.

By the time she'd gotten Shoogles, the property had changed hands, so she asked the new guy for permission to do the same.

"Sure, no problem."

"Great, thanks."

Then one day, he stomped toward her passing kayak (she let Shoogles out only when there was no one there, that was the deal), with belligerence written all over his body and called out to her, angrily. She stopped. Took off her headphones. He told her she couldn't let her dog out any more at his place.

Oh. That would be a disappointment. For both of them.

"May I ask why?"

"Yeah, because you let it shit all over the place!"

"No," she was aghast, "I don't!" She would never—

"I've *seen* it!" he insisted.

"Well, I don't know what you saw, but it wasn't Shoogles's shit. And if she ever *did* shit at your place, I'd pick it up." That was also the deal. She rummaged in her kayak bag, then held up her retractable leash—it had several poop bags tied to the handle. She pointed at them. (Just in case.)

He was unconvinced.

"Why would I have enough respect to ask for your permission, then let her shit all over the place?" she asked. "That doesn't make sense."

He turned away.

The next time she paddled past, it occurred to her: he didn't know shit. What he was seeing was *goose* shit. (They *loved* his place: it was very grassy *and* an easy step up from the water.)

Since she acquiesced to his request (and Shoogles continued to shit in her favourite spot, at home, before they went kayaking), and since there no doubt continued to be shit all over the place, she assumed he'd eventually figure it out.

Or not.

The following summer, almost overnight the property became virtually unrecognizable: the cabin was replaced with a cottage, a shed, a garage, and two bunkies, and there appeared a dock, a sandy beach with a firepit, and a manicured lawn with a swing set. (Where do these people get the money from?) It became *Lakeside Fun*.

The lake's geese had apparently taken a few lessons from the wild turkeys who live in the area, because when a renter kid started throwing rocks at them (no doubt thinking that was lakeside fun), he was mobbed and required several stitches. That would explain the new little sign Vic saw when she passed by one day:

PLEASE
DO NOT
FEED THE GEESE!

It was, no doubt, intended to protect against future lawsuits. (Apparently, 'Do not feed' meant 'Do not throw rocks at'.) But it also implied that the guy thought the geese were coming onto his property only because, only when, the renters were feeding them (and was therefore a new occurrence).

Maybe he did eventually figure it out though, because the next time she passed by, she saw a dozen foil pie plates strung across the sand-grass line. (The geese just flew over it.) (They weren't *that* stupid.)

A week later, one of the renters tripped over the string, broke his arm, and sued the owner.

Apparently, the following week, the owner showed up in a rage ready to deal with the problem once and for all. Fortunately (or unfortunately, depending on who you're rooting for), he was from the city and so wasn't armed with a shotgun. Furthermore, in his rage, he failed to notice that the flock that day consisted not of geese, but of wild turkey. Hard to miss the difference, really: wild turkey have spurs on their heels, their talons are longer, their beaks are pointier, and they stand, oh, about groin-high. (So no one's quite sure what he thought he'd achieve with just a butterfly net.)

Next time Vic paddled past, she saw another little sign on the yard:

FOR SALE

One of the never-ending renovation projects, sending the sound of nail guns and power drills and circular saws echoing across the entire lake, was conducted by the new owner of *Serenity*. One day, when Vic turned the corner to paddle up the little creek (still the prettiest stretch on the whole lake; still Crown land on both sides), she was dismayed to see a new dock stretching across the entire width of the creek. Okay, the asshole with the quad-jetslam could no longer get past and into the creek, but neither could she.

She sat there fuming, until she noticed the guy must have been determined to use all and only natural materials. He'd cut and debarked eight birch trees, all nice and folksy, to use as dock supports.

Satan Takes Over

The beaver couldn't believe their good fortune.

As a postscript, Vic sent a note to the owner of *Serenity* suggesting that he take advantage of his location: "You could promote a 'Swim with the Beaver' thing, the Canadian equivalent of 'Swim with a Dolphin'!" (Had she also said that a beaver was essentially a fifty-pound rat? A furry crocodile? No. And see, that's the problem with message systems that have a word limit.) And so, oblivious to the obvious, he did as she'd suggested. (And one drunk and obnoxious renter, even more oblivious to the obvious, took him up on his offer.)

S peaking of which ...
    One mother of three, renting at *The Family Cottage*, and just wanting a little peace and quiet, suggested to her kids that they could paint the turtles! That'll be fun, right? She got them set up on the beach with little pots of paint, in red, yellow, and orange, and short, stubby paintbrushes, one for each of them, so no bickering, okay?

Then she headed back to her lounge chair, settled in with a huge sigh, a drink in one hand, a book in the other ...

Not only did she not realize that 'painted turtles' didn't mean *actually* painted, she didn't realize that 'snapping turtles' were quite a different species.

Fortunately, none of the kids was going to become a concert pianist anyway.

Unfortunately, the owner had put the word 'safe' on the rental webpage because he'd spent a fortune making a family-friendly swimming area, clearing away all the rocks and anchoring a string of colourful pool noodles to mark the perimeter of the shallow part.

So the parents sued for misrepresentation. And, of course, personal injury.

Perhaps having finally read one of Vic's many letters, the one pointing out that Canada was #1 in the world for total garbage per person, the Township implemented a waste disposal fee, a per pound charge for garbage brought to the dump. (Though that may have been motivated more by their having run out of room than by a concern for the environment.) Not a bad idea. In theory.

In practice, a bunch of near-bursting garbage bags started appearing on the Township roads every Sunday afternoon. Coincidence? Guess so.

Then bears and raccoons started appearing on the Township roads every Sunday evening. Coincidence? Guess so.

Then bears and raccoons started appearing on the Township roads every Sunday afternoon. Renters on their way back to the city thought it was a wonderful end to their stay. A selfie with a bear!

Then torn up renters started appearing on the Township roads every Monday morning.

Eventually the Township put two and two together. And got five. They closed the dump on Sundays.

(Pity, Vic thought, you can't sue for stupidity.)

O n a few rare occasions, someone else stepped up ...
Early on, it was fashionable for jetslammers to spray people who were sitting on their docks. (Despite it being illegal to drive over 10 kmh within 100 feet of shore.)

"Why do you do that?" Vic asked one of them when his machine stalled in front of her dock, after he'd sprayed the people at the next dock.

"What?"

"Why do you spray people who are just sitting on their docks."

"I don't know," he smiled, "I guess I figure I owe it to myself to have a little fun now and then."

"How do you figure that?"

"What?"

"What is the basis for that obligation you claim?"

"What?"

"You said you *owe* it to yourself to have fun. Not just that you *want* to have fun."

Silence.

"There's a difference."

Silence.

"Furthermore, how do you figure you're entitled to have fun at other people's expense?"

He restarted his machine and drove off, too confused, apparently, to spray her.

Next time it happened, the guy at the next dock whipped a rock at the jetslammer. A big rock.

How quickly fashions change.

And see, that illustrates just one of the many problems— Thanks to collusion between the real estate agent industry and the region's Townships (who mistake themselves for Chambers of Commerce and citizens for consumers, and so understand progress to mean someone's financial gain), all waterfront property is called 'recreational' instead of 'residential'—presumably 'recreation' is more attractive than 'residence' and somehow generates more money). Despite the residences on waterfront property. More to the point, despite the residents on waterfront property.

The guy who rented *Our Summer Home* in mid-July must've done so only so 'the wife and kids' would 'shut up' because he spent the entire time down on the sandy beach swinging golf balls into the lake. There must've been hundreds of them at the bottom of the lake by the time he was done.

Mid-week, there was yet another middle-of-the-night middle-of-the-lake party. This time, one of the congregated boats, all brightly lit, contained someone who had figured out how to power his mobile dj system—'mobile' being the key word here—with a car battery. (And yes, someone, no doubt the person who had to get up for work in the morning, had no doubt called the O.P.P. at one o'clock, and again at *two*, and again at THREE, and again at *FOUR*, but the O.P.P. had hundreds of such parties to attend to, there being hundreds of lakes in the area, each with at least one rental ...) (And the problem was that most renters had the 'We paid $7,000 for the week, we're going to do whatever the fuck we want!' attitude.) (Admittedly, most occupants of the multi-family cottages had a similar attitude: they were there just for the week, so WOO-HOO!)

Suddenly, the party stopped. Well, not suddenly, but over the course of ten consecutive and discrete moments. It was as if each of the ten teenagers on board were controlled by a remote on-off switch.

And then, in the heavenly silence, someone called out *"FOUR!"*

Or maybe it was *"FORE!"*

E very rental had a 'Welcome Packet'—a binder of laminated pages listing important phone numbers, wifi and netflix passwords, cottage rules, and 'things to do' and 'places to see'. One of the suggested things to do at *The Family Cottage* was to go berry picking. The owner had conveniently included a small map, indicating a wild raspberry patch near the end of the path that led to the snowmobile trail.

So on a nice, sunny day, Grandma (fit at sixty!), the seven-year-old, and the nine-year-old headed into the bush via the marked path. It seemed like a delightful path. Just wide enough for the three of them, twisting and turning through the thick forest ...

The path wasn't part of the designated 40,000 kilometres of trails that Ontario had put aside for the exclusive use of snowmobilers and ATVers (without consulting the hikers, dogwalkers, skiers, and snowshoers who had been using the trails), but since ATVs *can* go everywhere, they *do*. (Apparently, 40,000 kilometres aren't enough.) At Paradise Lake, they especially go on the path that led to the snowmobile trail. Over time, the weight of the machines compacted the soil beyond its capacity to absorb water. So when it rained, where the ground was level, the water just sat there in huge muddy puddles; where the ground sloped, the water ran off, taking the top soil with it, leaving a mess of exposed roots and rocks.

So no wonder the seven-year-old tripped and fell. She picked up her bucket, and they carried on.

A hundred metres later, the nine-year-old tripped and fell. He picked up his bucket, and they carried on.

And then Grandma tripped and fell. She damn near— She picked up her bucket, and they carried on.

And then an ATV roared up behind them. Grandma grabbed the two kids, eyes darting to the left and the right, looking for a break, an opening, but there really wasn't one, and in their rush to get off the path—the ATV driver *had* stopped, just in time, but was revving his engine in impatience—all three of them tripped and fell. The seven-year-old and the nine-year-old learned some new words, and then they carried on.

After two more ATVs raced toward and then away from them, Grandma had a headache from the fumes, the seven-year-old was still bleeding, and the nine-year-old was still limping.

Quick learners, as soon as they *heard* the fourth ATV, which meant it was still a several kilometres away (yes: let it be known that ATVs create a corridor of noise eight kilometres wide), they started watching for a bit of a clearing, came across one several metres ahead, and left the path at that point, going considerably further into the bushery than was absolutely necessary.

Good thing. Because the fifth ATV approached at the same time. From the other direction. Of course, the two drivers didn't hear each other over their own engines. And they couldn't see each other because of the twist and turns. (One might think that would have affected their speed, but … no.) It was a spectacular head-on collision.

Next day, Grandma drove them into the forest a little ways on an old logging road, then parked so they could get out and have a pleasant walk to the other berry patch marked on the little map. She didn't know that in Ontario, it's pretty much hunting season all year long, and people—who are almost always men—have the right to shoot at shit all year long. (Bear, deer, and moose were limited to certain weeks, but it was always open season on squirrels, rabbits, raccoons, and coyotes, for example.) They're not supposed to shoot at people, but who can see as far as a bullet can travel?

She also didn't know that the old sand pit was often used for target practice. Typically by local men, often with their young sons, killing defenceless creatures being a rite of passage to manhood. (Go figure.) (No, seriously. One could figure out the world from that starting point.)

At the first gunshot, they wisely (given the likely position of the target, relative to the road) (and the likely presence of beer) turned and ran. Back to their car. Back to *The Family Cottage*.

Next day, Grandma decided they'd just walk on the road—not the logging road, but the road that led in to Paradise Lake. There were no berry patches along the road, but it was still pretty, and there was, according to the 'Welcome Packet', a little waterfalls half a mile from the cottage.

The first pick-up to pass them sprayed gravel in their faces. The seven-year-old started to cry. The nine-year-old started to cry. Grandma taught them a few more new words.

Grandpa left a detailed comment—a commentary, actually—in the 'Guest Book' part of the Welcome Packet. And on the cottage webpage.

The owner printed the commentary, took it to the next Association meeting, and proposed that they petition the Township to petition the Ministry to provide just *one* trail at Paradise Lake on which motorized vehicles were prohibited (and, ideally, men with guns). Fifteen signatures would represent 50% of the Lake's taxpayers, so surely—

Five of the owners were in agreement, five didn't really care one way or the other, and five were NO FUCKING WAY! OUR RENTERS COME HERE TO HAVE FUN, AND EVERYONE HAS A

RIGHT TO USE CROWN LAND, WE ALL PAY TAXES, GOD DAMN IT, SO THEY CAN DO WHATEVER THEY WANT!

"Not these two," the owner of *The Family Cottage* slid the medical examiner's report across the table. "Not anymore."

That may have been their last meeting.

C learly showing poor judgment and lack of forethought, and as likely, not knowing that Paradise Lake was full of slightly submerged trees and stumps, the new owner of *Lakeside Fun* provided several round rubber dinghy things that could be towed behind a jetslam or motor boat, should their renters bring one. Oh what fun!

And oh what a supremely stupid idea! The kids had no control whatsoever over where they were going, round rubber dinghy things having no steering capability whatsoever. Unlike, say, old-fashioned water skis, with their grooves and rudders.

So why didn't the owner provide a pair of water skis instead? Because it would take a kid half a dozen tries to get up. And another half a dozen tries to stay up. Dare I make a comment about today's kids? Their inability to persist in the face of difficulty? Their inability to *practice* something until they get it right? (It's called *learning.*) There's a reason Asians dominate, relative to their population size, American and Canadian symphony orchestras. (And it's not a race thing; it's a culture thing.)

In theory, the kids could bail, especially if they were wearing life jackets, but most of the time, they were going so fast, they couldn't even see what was coming. (Which was, perhaps, a good thing.)

The same could not be said for the drivers of said jetslams or motor boats.

Or the owner of *Lakeside Fun.*

Understandably, sometimes posting feedback on the rental webpage was not enough: several distraught parents sued the owner for failure to warn and for the provision of unsafe toys.

S peaking of which, one Saturday afternoon, along the narrow stretch of river, a hot shot slalom skier, probably one of the many young men staying at *Weekend Getaway,* was clearly showing all the locals how it's done. He was cutting back and forth over the boat's wake using exposed stumps as buoys, and Vic, parked safely in the marsh for the duration, had to say he really knew what he was doing: decelerating as he approached a stump, then letting go with one hand and leaning, leaning, to slice a curve around it, then grabbing on again and pulling hard, picking up speed as he crossed the wake, so much speed that when he hit the (barely) *submerged* stump, he flew. Landed on the road. (Jocks.)

Unfortunately he landed right in front of an oncoming ATV. The bright yellow one. The one driven by the asshole who'd screamed at Vic one day "'YA GOTTA GET OUT OF MY WAY, LADY!'", the one who apparently didn't know how to steer or brake.

Pedestrians don't always have the right of way and, arguably, the slalom guy wasn't a pedestrian at the moment anyway. (And, sadly, wasn't likely to be one in the future.)

Still.

His family sued the rental owner for not providing a warning in the 'Welcome Packet', the Township for not removing all the dead trees and stumps from the river, and the ATV asshole for being an asshole.

A nd then there were the sky lanterns. Essentially, candles in paper bags. The owner of *Peace and Love* kept a box full inside the cottage, a complimentary thing, like firewood bundles or scented soaps. The renters of *Peace and Love* liked to set them adrift over the lake. The key word here is 'adrift'. One evening, every one of them adrifted over to *The Family Cottage*, which was on the other side. And occupied at the time by two families.

The eighteen-year-old, understanding that trees were flammable, thought to call 9-1-1. While he ran around trying to find a signal, screaming "Fuck Rogers!" (or maybe it was "Fuck Bell!" or "Fuck Telus!") (or possibly all three ...), the sixteen-year-old, with similar understanding, powered up her laptop to use Skype to make the call. Apparently she's still waiting for the program update to download (a process she couldn't abort) because internet speed at Paradise Lake, whether you use Rogers or Bell—Telus doesn't even bother—is often *under* 1.0 mbps.) (And it costs $60 for a whole 5GB. At *under* 1.0 mbps. Did I say that already?)

The other four teenagers, orchestrated by the Moms, each filled a pail with water and stationed themselves around the property. As soon as a branch was ignited, then fell to the ground, they doused it, stomped on it, then ran down to the lake for another pail of water.

"So pretty ... " crooned the people over at *Peace and Love.* It's possible the owner also left a box full of special gummies.

Fortunately, only one whole tree ignited. Unfortunately, it was the one over the propane tank. Fortunately, one of the Dads remembered seeing a hose and outdoor tap at the neighbouring house. He ran over, unwound the hose, turned the tap on full, ran back dragging the hose behind him, then stood watering the propane tank. Half an hour later, when the Fire Department still hadn't shown up (the carrier duck was tired that day), they all just made a run for it.

Both Dads at *The Family Cottage* demanded a refund, of course, and vowed never to return. Not messin' around with a petition this time, the owner of *The Family Cottage* sued the renters at and the owner of *Peace and Love* for loss of income and damages (the tank did eventually explode in a most spectacular fashion). He also sued the Fire Department for not showing up "in a timely fashion". And the Township for not having a 'No-Setting-Adrift-Candles-in-Paper-Bags' bylaw. And the teenagers sued Bell, Rogers, Telus, and Skype. For shitty service. (Oh, and the next door neighbour, a renter, sued the Dad for trespassing.)

And that seemed to open the gates ...

One of the worst of the seven permanent residences, as far as Vic was concerned, was the one with the recently retired couple. One would think 'quiet' but—

First, the bickering. It was constant. It was loud. The two of them couldn't stand to be around each other all day. And had, apparently, just discovered this.

Second, retired men are forever having to *do* something, they're always *outside* with their little projects, their far too numerous landscape maintenance machines, their far too numerous power tools. All day long. And into the evening. And the night. (The guy had installed several outdoor work lights.)

My god, there were birdhouses, treehouses, gazebo tables, patio furniture ... The guy had built all of that *and* fourteen little sheds. (In additional to his almost daily use of either a lawnmower, a weed trimmer, or a leaf blower, the latter, sadly, not yet illegal on Paradise Lake, despite being so in hundreds of other places, land-locked places ...) (Perhaps the Township of Paradise Lake doesn't know that a single two-stroke leaf blower is 300 times more polluting than a truck and as noisy as a chainsaw.) (More likely, they don't care.) (More likely still, they just *love* their trucks, *and* noise ...)

Why couldn't the retired guy just sit in his fucking gazebo or on his fucking patio and, I don't know, do crossword puzzles? Read? Knit?

He was not that kind of man. He was the kind of man who believed that being active meant you were still alive. And goddammit, *he was still alive!*

And, as fate would have it, *Tranquility Cottage* was on the adjacent property.

Six renters in a row sued the owner for misrepresentation and demanded a refund.

Finally, the owner sued the retired guy for loss of income. And unreasonable interference with use and enjoyment of property.

It was nothing new for Vic to see garbage while she paddled, but with the arrival of the rentals, there was just that much more of it. She used to collect it—water bottles, beer cans, bait containers, bits of styrofoam—and take it all back with her to put into her trash can for her next trip to the dump.

But when she retrieved a small plastic chair from the lake (she drew the line at retrieving the rusted barrel she saw), she started leaving whatever she picked up at the nearest developed property, so *they* could put it in *their* trash can for *their* next trip to the dump. After all, keeping the lake clean, free of garbage, was everyone's responsibility.

But now she just left it all at Trailer Park #2. And appropriately so. Because in addition to the three can-be-occupied trailers, the two collapsed trailers, the abandoned pick-up, the half-ATV, various snowmobile parts, and a great deal of unidentifiable shit, there was now a dumpster. On the property.

That was, apparently, the last straw for the owner of *Our Summer Home*, the rental across the way. He asked, nicely, whether they couldn't've put it behind the trees, out of sight. As he had asked before regarding the two collapsed trailers, the abandoned pick-up, the half-ATV, the various snowmobile parts, and—he'd gestured vaguely at the unidentifiable shit.

The trailer park guy's response was the same as it had been before: "Fuck off, you fuckin' cunt, FUCK!" (Vic would've had mixed thoughts about that response: delight at the now non-sexist application of the worst insult ever; dismay that the worst insult ever was, still, essentially female.)

So, the owner of *Our Summer Home* sued the owner of Trailer Park #2. For loss of income, past, present, and future.

T he day after the owner of *Chillin' at the Lake* finished building his luxury rental, after two years and two million dollars, he happily posted it on the most popular cottage rental portal, highlighting the million-dollar view—indeed, nothing but water and forest—giddily anticipating the $10,000/ week bookings that would roll in ...

As soon as the champagne stopped bubbling, he saw some action across the lake. What? He'd been told it was Crown land. (Yeah. And he'd assumed, correctly, probably, that they'd never log waterfront. But he hadn't been told that the Ministry could *sell* Crown land for development ...)

First, they clear-cut the trees. Then they levelled the lot, uprooting all the weeds and wild grass and trilliums and tiger lilies, which left just ... dirt.

He watched nervously. Maybe it would be a golf course. That would be good. In fact, a golf course right across from his luxury rental would be great.

A shipping container appeared. What the hell?

He immediately contacted the Township. Had the zoning laws been changed? Was the lot across from his luxury rental now available, oh god, for industrial use?

"What?" said the clerk.

"Zoning laws?" said the mayor.

Then another shipping container appeared. And another.

And then people appeared. They appeared to move in. They were going to *live* in those things? Apparently. By the end of the week, the guy's luxury rental looked out across the water to a shipping container villa.

Well, talk about a neighbourhood with diversity.

He went back to the Township. Were they allowed? Apparently. They were just a version of trailer parks.

Of course, when lots are wide enough and on waterfront, their centers should be staggered so the people in one house aren't looking across at the people in another house, but at their (hopefully) beautiful bits of forest on either side of the house. Or, the owner of *Chillin' at the Lake* thought, the owners of such lots should build not in the center of their lots, but at the edges. Well, too late now. What he *really* should have done was *buy* the lot across from the one he developed. No, wait, he'd been told it was Crown land. (And he hadn't been told that the Crown could sell it ...)

(So now you know ... when 40 of the 50 photos on the rental webpage show the *inside* of the house, 5 photos show close-ups of the yard, the beach, and the docks, and the other 5 show views of the area *from somewhere else*, expect the view *from the rental property* to be of a bunch of shipping containers.)

At first, paddling past, Vic had that thought they were dumpsters, but on her next paddle, she'd seen that they were, indeed, shipping containers. Ugly-as-shit shipping containers. Parked on a waterfront lot, a beautiful Algonquin-Park-like waterfront lot, because ... Because they were cheaper than a cabin, an RV, and a trailer? And sturdier than a tent? But, so—people were going to *live* there? Willingly?

Apparently. Because next time she paddled past, there were nine people there.

And then there were none.

Turned out that during the subsequent heat wave, they all went inside one of the containers for the shade, pulled the door closed, and *then* discovered that said door didn't open from the inside.

Great, Vic thought. Now those shipping containers will sit there, for all of eternity.

Or at least until there's a new owner. Who's not into shipping containers.

Until then, a family of bears moved into one of them. Not the greatest caves they'd ever occupied, but the mattresses were nice. And there was a steady supply of food next door. Meals were even announced with the banging of pots and pans. How cool was that?

Raccoons quickly took over a second one. Take-out right next door all night long.

Turns out there was no new owner. The lot *was* Crown land. And the owner of *Chillin'* discovered, with considerable dismay, that anyone can camp pretty much anywhere on Crown land, for free, for up to 21 days; then they just need to move 100 metres and can stay another 21 days; then they just need to move again, presumably back to the first place if they want, and stay another 21 days ... True, you can't cut down trees on Crown land, let alone level it, but, well, too late now. (He also discovered that every local who had a pick-up had a chainsaw, and probably knew someone who had an excavator.)

So, eternity it was, thought Vic with a sigh, thinking of the dump of refrigerators two miles in behind her cabin, still there, on Crown land, after thirty years. She passed it every time she went for a walk in the forest.

Or not. The owner of *Chillin'* threatened to sue the Ministry for loss of income. (The first renters had posted a picture on the rental webpage, and well, no one wanted to pay $10,000 to look at a bunch of shipping containers for a week.) (Indeed, thought Vic.)

They were gone in a day. (*A day.*)

Vic was stunned. Then enraged. Because the *Taylor's* shit, now including old bed springs, was still across from her property, still spoiling *her* million-dollar view ...

Which just goes to show.

But even without the shipping containers, the view had been compromised. So the owner sued the Ministry for failure to protect its property against vandalism leading to depreciation of another's property. Essentially, for loss of future income.

The Ministry couldn't, in turn, sue the people who'd set up the shipping container villa because, well, they were dead. And had no estate to speak of. (Surprise.)

Satan Takes Over

The damages were huge, because it was, after all, a permanent destruction, a permanent depreciation. (Well, perhaps not *permanent*, but it would take a hundred years, at least, for the beauty to return.) The owner of *Chillin'* had, for a moment, considered buying the land, should the Ministry agree to sell it, but, yeah, the trees were down. And anyway, the rule was, as he understood it, that Crown land could be sold for *development*. Not for preservation. (Go figure.)

So then he thought, okay, he could *develop* it into a golf course. Revenue from that would offset the loss of future rental income, so the Ministry would have an interest in facilitating that development, as it would reduce the damages claimed in the suit. But the optics, as they say, would be horrendous: "Ministry sells waterfront Crown forest for private golf course sure to kill the ecosystem with fertilizer run-off"! (Of course, "Ministry sells Crown lots to aid munipalities' economic development" is, in truth, no different, but ... truth?

When the owner of *The Family Cottage* found out what had happened, he joined the conga line and followed up on his petition to the Ministry with threats to sue for loss of future income for as long as ATVs and snowmobiles were allowed on the path at Paradise Lake.

Two days later, there was a sign at the entrance to the path prohibiting all motorized vehicles.

A week later, the owner of *The Party Place* sued the Ministry for loss of future income for as long as ATVs and snowmobiles were *not* allowed on the path at Paradise Lake.

Clearly the Ministry had some thinking to do. Because if everyone was allowed to do whatever they want on Crown land, everyone would not be able to do whatever they want on Crown land. For anyone who's taken Philosophy 101, it was a variation on the tragedy of the commons, and so a basic premise in the argument for limits on freedoms when living in society. For the Ministry, it was a philosophical conundrum they simply could not wrap their heads around.

Regardless, Vic gave serious consideration to renting out her beloved cabin. For just a week or so, just long enough to establish loss of future income, due to, oh, a number of things ...

Most of the rentals at Paradise Lake didn't allow pets at all, and the ones that did almost always had limits of number and weight. (What, no such limits on the kids that are allowed?) A typical limit was something like 'No more than two dogs, each weighing no more than 25 pounds.' But a lot of people who want to rent a cottage have 40-pound dogs. Some even have 80-pound dogs. *Rover's Retreat* advertised that it was 'pet-friendly' and had no limits. So it was, among all of the rentals, the most booked. The people who rented it during the third week of July had 100-pound dogs. Three of them. A black Newfoundland, a brown-and-white St. Bernard, and a multi-colour who-knows-what.

Many dogs, upon hearing fireworks, or thunder, hide under the bed quivering for the duration. Others tear around outside barking, presumably trying to make the monster go away. Still others just take off—RUN AWAY! RUN AWAY! In this case, it was door number three.

There had been fireworks every night for a week, thanks to one of the trailer parks, but the renters of *Rover's Retreat* would not have known that, since they'd just arrived that day. And they would not have expected that, since it was not a holiday weekend.

So when the fireworks began, the dogs were not safely inside the house. Yes, they were inside the fenced area, but it was only four feet high.

So ... when the fireworks began, the dogs zoomed around the enclosure a couple times to gain speed, then cleared the fence (which, honestly, at 100-pounds, was impressive, and Vic was sorry she'd she'd missed seeing that) and went tearing down the road in the dark. And none of them had on its reflective collar with the blinkey lights.

The good news is that the dogs didn't get hit by the ATV roaring down the middle of the road. (Perhaps it too was running away from the fireworks.) The driver saw the pack of wolves heading straight for him and went hysterical. He drove off the road. And kept going. Hit a tree. A very big tree. Stopped at that point.

The dogs might have assumed the ATV was the source of attack. And reasonably so. Instead, they just kept running. Because the fireworks continued. (Clearly they were the more rational.)

Their owners spent the night looking for them, calling them ...

Once the fireworks were over, at around 2 a.m., the trailer park people were annoyed at hearing two people calling out "Tulip",

"Daffodil", and "Jelly Bean" over and over and over, so they called the O.P.P. There were noise bylaws after all.

They finally found the dogs at 4 a.m., safe and sound. At Vic's place. Shoogles had alerted her to their presence at the gate, at around 3:00 a.m., and when she went out to let them in, they emptied Shoogles's outdoor water pail, three times, accepted the snacks Vic offered, then headed straight for her shed (her new shed—the old one had partly fallen in and partly fallen over) and, exhausted, made themselves at home. Sweet. (At 4 a.m., Shoogles alerted her again to their presence at the gate, hearing their names being called, the owners having returned to Paradise Lake Lane, after going halfway to town on Paradise Lake Road ...)

The renters sued the owner for breach of contract and emotional distress (theirs *and* the dogs'). Pet-friendly, my ass! The owner sued the trailer park people for disturbing the peace. They also sued the Township for not having a 'No-Fireworks-Except-on-Designated-Holidays-and-Only-Between-10 p.m.-and-11 p.m.' bylaw.

The trailer park people contested. At first, she wondered how poor trailer trash could afford a lawyer for what was likely to be a long drawn-out affair, but then she remembered that trailer park people aren't necessarily poor (or trash). If they'd bought a used Hyundai instead of a new pick-up, they could've sent their kids to university.

And then there was the paddleboard incident. One of the teenagers of one of the two families renting *TGIF* went for a paddle. It was his first time, so he stayed, as his parents had suggested, close to shore. He refused to wear a life jacket though, because that was just so not cool. By the time he'd passed the third dock, he was getting the hang of it. And then he paddled into a mess of spiderwebs. AARGH!

No, not spiderwebs. Fishing lines. The guy at *Gone Fishin'*, no doubt thinking that 'all the fish you can eat' meant 'caught at the lake', not 'bought at the buffet in town' (supplied by the grocery store across the road), had set up six lines on the dock, like an overly optimistic bingo player (though with considerably worse odds) (despite using this year's highly recommended 'Super Duper 12-Prong Nasty-Barbed Lures').

(And see, right there: a perfect illustration of the bigger problem. Yes, there were twenty times as many people at the lake, but the impact was *ten times* twenty. Because someone actually living at Paradise Lake might cast just *one* fishing line. Might drive on the road just *once a week*. Might go to the dump just *once every two weeks*. And so on.) (Though, to be honest, someone living at Paradise Lake would know there are no fish, because, so …)

The *Gone Fishin'* guy was, at the critical moment, inside the cottage getting another beer.

By the time everything got untangled, and unhooked—it's impossible to stop a paddleboard on a dime, so to speak—the teenager had lost both eyes. (The guy had reeled in one line so quickly, it tore the young man's eye right out of its socket.) Worse, or not, one of his testicles got sliced off. (When taut, a fishing line is a cross between a garrote and a guillotine.)

So, yeah, the *TGIF* parents sued the *Gone Fishin'* guy. For obvious reasons.

Vic didn't think paddleboards would last—they were too hard on the back—and she was right. But she hadn't anticipated what would take its place: jetboards. Spawn of jetslams and paddleboards. Though, thankfully, they were powered by an electric motor rather than a two-stroke engine. So there were no fumes, no fuel going into the water, and, Vic had to admit, their whine wasn't quite as bad as that of a jetslam. Furthermore, maneuvering them took more skill than maneuvering either a jetslam or a paddleboard.

Unfortunately, they took so much skill, few mastered the ride. Most weren't even close.

Five collided with a paddleboard. No surprise there.

Four collided with a jetslam. Surprise there, I'll bet.

Three collided with one of the dozens of dead trees and stumps variously exposed or submerged throughout the lake and river, depending on the water level and the wind. An attentive person who lived at the lake and kayaked every day knew where each one of these were. Renters had no idea they existed. Even if, apparently, they were clearly visible.

Two collided with a dock. Not necessarily the one they were aiming for.

And one collided with a shore. That one sued the Township. Because, what, the shore shouldn't have been there? Because there should've been a warning sign saying "CAUTION: THE LAWS OF PHYSICS PREDICT EJECTION UPON IMPACT"?

Speaking of which ...

Everyone was surprised when the first bullet-shaped 'cigarette' boat appeared on Paradise Lake. Because seriously, it was barely a lake. 'A bulge at the end of a narrow river' was more accurate.

One problem with such boats is that at full-throttle, they can go from zero to sixty in four seconds flat. Which meant they could go from one end of the lake to the other in about 30 seconds. Well, that was fun.

Yeah, I'm bored now.

Let's do it again.

And again.

The other problem is that at full-throttle, pretty much the entire boat is lifted out of the water at an angle. Which means the occupants can't see where they're going.

Which explains why the Taylors don't have a dock anymore. All gone! (Yay!)

(Reportedly, at a certain speed, ejection into bedsprings is like ejection into razor wire.)

And then there was the guy who brought his yacht to Paradise Lake. Only he knew why. Scratch that. He's probably not that self-aware. He had to park it—anchor it—some distance from the dock of the rental he was staying at, *Our Summer Home*, thereby blocking the promised view of the sunset for the people who'd rented *Sunset Haven* (and, by the way, everyone who lived on Sunset Lane). Since they'd paid over $3,000 to *see* the sunset, they asked for a full refund (sending a picture of 'the sunset') to support their request. Once they had their money in hand, they sued the owner for misrepresentation. Of course, in turn, the owner sued the yacht guy (the picture had shown the yacht's registration number) for loss of income.

One late afternoon while paddling back, Vic saw a bunch of white blobs floating in the lake in front of *The Party Place.* Oh no, she thought before she realized there hadn't been that many baby geese and baby loons on the lake. Nor even that many fish, baby or otherwise. When she got closer, she realized they were ... potatoes? What the hell?

Something hit her in the head. Unfortunately, she lost consciousness. Fortunately, the cold water she fell into revived her instantly. Unfortunately her kayak had started to drift away. Fortunately Shoogles, who couldn't swim, was still in it. Unfortunately, Shoogles also couldn't paddle.

"DOWN!" she yelled as another potato went whizzing by at the speed of—potatoes thrown by the Hulk?

She dove, came up beside her kayak, saw with great relief that Shoogles was huddled well under the prow, then managed to use the kayak as a shield as she made her way out of range.

When she got home, she googled. Using the search terms 'idiots' and 'potatoes'.

And she read that "A potato cannon"—a fucking what?—"is a

pipe-based cannon that uses air pressure (pneumatic) or combustion of a flammable gas (aerosol, propane, etc.) to launch projectiles at high speeds. They are built to fire chunks of potato, as a hobby." Unfortunately there was no link from the word 'hobby' to indicate what definition of the word they were using.

She also read that recent research found that if you're hit in the head with a potato, you have more than a 50% risk of skull fracture. "Even taking a body shot could do some serious damage and has a good chance of killing you." And these things were legal? Men.

She considered suing, but without evidence, it would be her word against theirs. Been there, done that. Like every woman in the world. So, she just ... waited.

The very next day, she saw a hapless kayaker paddling into the line of fire. She grabbed her megaphone and screamed 'INCOMING!" The kid didn't respond, and might not have even if she hadn't had the voice still set to Alvin.

The family sued, of course. Long-term care for permanent brain damage was expensive. They named the renters, the owner, the Township, and the Ministry. (Happily, the presiding judges rejected their lawyer's defence, clearly stating that a reasonable person should *not* have foreseen the risk of being hit in the head with a potato while kayaking, including, but not limited to, a potato travelling at 80 kmh.)

S peaking of which ...
   A man and his two twenty-something sons arrived at *Tranquility Cottage* at 3 p.m., unloaded the car, unpacked

their stuff, and settled in. At 4 p.m., they heard gun shots. They were sure of it: both of the sons had served. (We support our troops.) (Thank you for your service.) (Gas is still under $5.00 per litre.) So they'd sure as hell know a gun shot from an engine backfire. The father got them both settled in front of the huge flat-screen tv, hoping it would distract them, but while he was online, discovering that the local gun club (there was a local gun club?) was using their nearby shooting range (there was shooting range nearby?) for their Saturday let's-get-together-and-practice-killing session, the brothers had started shooting back. It was a reasonable response.

They'd seen the muzzle flash across the lake, so that's where they aimed. Between them, they had 4 Norinco M14s (semi-automatics), 3 SKSs (predecessor to the AK47), 2 BRS-99s (a sort of Polish Uzi), and a seemingly endless supply of ammunition.

The father knew he couldn't, as the PTSD counsellor had advised, talk them into the here and now, because in the here and now there *were* gun shots. *Real* gun shots. *Six per second.*

So, honestly, he just took cover. Downstairs in the entertainment center. It was a reasonable response.

At 6 p.m., when the brothers heard that almost-unique 'incoming missile' whine, they got out their own rocket launcher.

Of course none of the permanent residents called the police because they heard hours of gunshot *every* Saturday. And every Thursday. (That's when the club had a potluck supper afterward.) And every— Well, the owner of the shooting range had insisted, when Vic had contacted him, that he had the right to be open 24/7. Like a convenience store. (She'd suggested fixed and limited hours, better berms, an indoor range, an underground range, she'd even suggested silencers. The owner had laughed at that last one. Actually, he'd laughed at all of her suggestions, but when she'd suggested silencers, a solution she thought was so ... obvious, he snorted and said 'The guys'll never go for that, they *like* the noise.') And as for the missile shriek, wasn't that fireworks? One of those whistling screamer ones? Again, no need to call the police.

Things got quiet at around 8 p.m. While the brothers watched a movie, the father sent emails to the owner of *Tranquility Cottage*, to the gun club president, to the shooting range owner, and to the Township. Had they even *done* an acoustic audit? Before giving a permit for a *shooting* range to be so established close to a waterway that was *an acoustic nightmare*, the river opening up to the lake like a tunnel opens up to a cave? Not to mention a waterway on which hundreds of people had their homes? He contacted a lawyer to sue for misrepresentation. And emotional distress. And reckless zoning.

They left bright and early the next morning. Because who knew when it would start again? Because 24/7.

Someone did eventually call the police. The wife of one of the trailer park guys. He hadn't come home late Sunday night like usual. Eight bodies were found. (And, on a picnic table, a shattered flat-screen, its shards still glinting in the sun.) By then, the bodies were pretty mangled by bear, wolves, coyotes, raccoons, beaver, and snapping turtles. Picked clean, actually. So there were no gunshot wounds to be noted. No bullets to be sought. No suspects to be identified. And no charges to be laid.

nd so it wasn't just the rentals.

Almost every day, someone drove into the ditch. Were they drunk? Had they been reckless? Possibly. But look: there were three dead-end lanes that, in all, provided access to waterfront properties. And they were indeed lanes. And that used to be okay. (Still was, as far as Vic was concerned. Widening or paving would just *increase* use.) Because with just one or two people living on each lane, what were the odds that someone would be driving out at exactly the same time someone else was driving in? And in that unlikely event, all you had to do was go carefully, slowly, while passing each other—because the lanes were actually, though barely, wide enough for two cars.

But now? The permanent residences had one, maybe two, cars. The rentals often had three to five cars. (One resident reported *six* vehicles at a next-door rental. And this was during the COVID lockdown.) And the trailer parks often had three to five pick-ups, the ones that were half-again as wide as a car, each with a double-wide trailer for their ATVs, jetslams, and/or snowmobiles.

As mentioned, someone who lived here might drive into town once a week. Not once a day. Certainly not several times a day.

And someone who lived here drove accordingly. The renters drove as if they were still in the city. No, actually, that's not true. Freed of stop signs and traffic lights every hundred metres, and lane markings, and other vehicles, they drove like they were the only ones on the road. The trailer park guys drove their pick-ups like they drove their ATVs and snowmobiles: like they *owned* the road, the trail, the forest. (Isn't that what the ads told them?) So when it became clear they *weren't* the only ones on the road, the other person had to drive into the ditch to avoid a head-on collision.

Satan Takes Over

One day, the guy in the ditch (one of the permanent residents) had a baseball bat with him. The guy in the pick-up (one of the trailer park guys) saw him coming and, anticipating a fight, opened his door, jumped out of the cab, and broke both his knees. (That's what happens to forty-five-year-old knees, already crumbling with the weight of a massive beer gut, when they hit the ground from a jacked-up six-foot drop.)

Even so, pick-up dude sued baseball-bat dude. 'Because if the other guy hadn't've had a baseball bat, he never would've gotten out of his truck.'   (What?)

The Dreshers had a beautiful house on a huge lot, one that could easily be mistaken for one of the 'sleeps twelve' rentals. And very often the late-night arrivals for *TGIF*, which was next door, would park in *their* driveway, come to *their* house, start feeling under *their* deck for the key, then start swearing because it wasn't there ... You'd think the frantic barking of Didi, the Dreshers' dog, would clue these people in to the fact that they had the wrong frickin' house, but ... no.

So the Dreshers put a helpful sign at the end of their driveway—**THIS IS NOT "*TGIF*"**—even mounting a motion and sound sensor light on top, but ... no.

So then they got one of those roll-out spike-strips and rolled it out across their driveway, about twenty feet past the helpful sign, every Friday afternoon. And stayed up late, with popcorn, giggling as they heard the tires pop ...

However, that didn't stop cars associated with *TGIF* from blocking their driveway. Which pretty much happened with every rental on the lake. Because few had driveway space for more than two cars. With trailers. And 'sleeps twelve' often meant three or four cars. With trailers.

Concerned about not being able to get out in case of emergency, residents living near rentals asked the Township to put up 'NO PARKING' signs, attaching a hefty fine for violations. The mayor said they'd discuss it at their next council meeting.

In the meantime, as it happened, an enterprising young woman with a tow truck found out about the problem (who knew how?) (Vic smiled) and approached the residents, offering her services. So every time it happened, they called her. She towed the cars to an undisclosed location and sent the towing bill to the address on the vehicle registration, which she tracked down using the license plate number.

Finding their vehicles missing, they went to the police, who, having coincidentally found abandoned vehicles that perfectly matched their descriptions, charged them, fined them, then billed them for the vehicles' release.

That worked quite nicely until there *was* an emergency. Not a life-threatening emergency, but an emergency nonetheless. (Deb missed the last step, went down hard on her hands and knees, possibly fracturing her wrist.) That day, there were cars parked on both sides of their driveway *and* along the other side (which was just bush). Technically, their driveway wasn't blocked, but since cars can't do 90 degree turns, Jim couldn't get out. By the time he got the people at the rental to move the car on the left side of his driveway so he *could* get out, Deb's wrist was three times its normal size and she was in a lot of pain ...

So Jim sued the Township. (And the renters and the rental owner.) Of course he did.

A year later, the Township widened the lane to enable parking on both sides. Not the expected, intended, result. Especially since the Township then increased everyone's property taxes to cover the road work. Sigh.

B ut it was mostly the rentals.

There were several—though not enough—jetslam vs. jetslam incidents. (To be expected when there are no 'rules of the road', no 'stay to the right', no lanes, no turn signals, no brake lights ... not that any of that would matter ...)

But only one jetslam vs. plane incident.

Yes, the plane had done a full circle overhead, indicating its intent to land (an inappropriate word, granted, given that it had pontoons and was going to 'land' on 'water'), and providing sufficient time for all motorboats, jetslams, jetboards, kayaks, canoes, paddleboats, rowboats, paddleboards, and swimmers to vacate the 'landing strip'. (You'd think this necessity would render Paradise Lake unsuitable for use as a 'landing strip' for pontoon planes, but no. Perhaps because the Township owned the airport. Presumably there was a per-plane use payment.)

That said, what made the *Jetslam v. Plane* suit particularly interesting was not only the involvement of the plaintiff, the defendant, the Township, the Ministry of Natural Resources, and the Ministry of Transport, but the involvement of, also, the Ministry of Agriculture. Apparently because of the numerous mentions by both the plaintiff and the defendant, in subsequent interviews, of 'chicken'.

T he webpage for *Peace and Love* promised starry skies, meteor showers, and fireballs. It was true that, relative to the city, Paradise Lake had little light pollution, so there *were* starry skies and the chance to see meteor showers and fireballs. Until the owner of *TGIF*, across from *Peace and Love,* installed several lights, lakeside. The owner of *Peace and Love* asked him, politely, if he could leave a note in his 'Welcome Packet' asking his renters to turn off the lights when they went to bed.

In response, the owner of *TGIF* added more lights.

So the owner of *Peace and Love* installed a spotlight aimed right at *TGIF*. A very big, very bright, on-all-night-long spotlight. He figured that would make his point.

In response, the owner of *TGIF* installed a veritable runway of spot lights. A very long, very bright runway, each light aimed up at the sky to make sure no stargazing was possible.

That's when the aliens saw it and used it for a landing.

Hah! No such luck. But a plane saw it.

And so ... *Plane v. House.*

I n early August, a renter posted on the *Serenity* webpage that it was not conducive to her serenity to see men kill animals. To see them jab a hook into the animal's mouth, then yank on that hook several times, then wind a reel to lift the animal up, up, up *by the hook in its mouth*— To see the animal jerking, flailing, as it suffocates, dying ... If fish could scream— She included a link to research that proved fish had pain receptors.

As far as Vic was concerned, the woman was absolutely right. 'Fishing' and 'hunting' were euphemisms to mask the simple (and horrible) truth: it was killing. Not in self-defence. Not out of mercy. For food? Please. Most of us do not have to resort to eating others in order to survive. People—mostly men—who were fishing and hunting were killing for fun. For sport. And she was sickened every time such a man taught his child that yes, it was okay, it was good, to inflict pain on others. You caught one!

The pictures the renter had posted weren't sufficient for identification, so the owner didn't know who to sue. He tried to have Paradise Lake declared a 'No Fishing' lake, but failed. He put 'NO FISHING' signs in the water in front of his house and in the marsh across from his house, but they were ignored. (He didn't own the lake!)

But when the owner of *Gone Fishin'* heard about the signs, he sued the owner of *Serenity*.

Well, now the owner of *Serenity* knew who to sue. For distress and cruelty to animals.

To Vic's surprise, not only did the judge rule in his favour, she (Ah. That explains it.) sent a strongly worded recommendation to the Ministry prohibiting the killing of fish in *any* provincial body of water. "Enabling psychopaths is bad enough," she reportedly wrote, "but enabling them to kill animals exactly when we should be doing everything we can to help them survive—habitat destruction and extinction rates being off the charts, thanks to global warming—is almost *as* psychopathic."

Vic cheered.

A similar post appeared on the *Tranquility Cottage* webpage. The trees along the shoreline had so many bright, shiny fishing lures in them, it seemed that every day some hapless squirrel or bird was snagged, strangled, or decapitated. And whether they tried to rescue them or just left them there, the renters noted, it wasn't very conducive to tranquility.

What was happening was the guys in their little fishing boats would park close to shore to fish, because that's where the non-existent fish were, and either incompetent or inattentive, they would cast high into the trees. The lure would get stuck in the tree. (Who'd've thought?) They'd pull a few times, to no avail. (Who'd've thought?) Then, instead of docking their boat, getting out, and climbing the tree to retrieve their stuck-and-tangled lure, they'd just cut the line and move on. Leaving the lure in the tree, a length of line taut among the branches, its end dangling in the breeze. For all eternity.

And as Vic could attest, the bright, shiny lures were not only a hazard for squirrels and birds, seeing them glinting in the sun among in the trees ruined the view.

So the owner ended up cutting half his trees. Not half of his trees; half of *each of* his trees. As a result, his property value and rental income decreased considerably. (A shoreline of trees with most of their lakeside limbs sawn off? Not the beautiful view he was charging his renters for.) (Nor, as he would discover, the solution he'd hoped for.) He asked the Township and the Ministry to prohibit fishing within 150 metres of private property. Staffed by men who kill, every one of them, both the Township and the Ministry refused.

So he sued both the Township and the Ministry.

And when he received several videos and close-up photographs (from a 'Bill Wordsworth'), he was able to sue several individuals as well.

And then there was the beach fiasco.

After laboriously cutting down all the shoreline trees, the owner of *Sunset Haven* had a truck load of sand delivered. After a good deal of raking, he had a beach. Some called it beautiful. (Others called it illegal: cutting down shoreline trees and dumping sand where none had been destroys the habitat. You know, what non-human animals call 'home'.)

The following summer, the sand was gone! So he had another truckload delivered.

The summer after that, that sand was gone too! And so he had yet another truckload delivered.

Finally, he noticed that the Fontaines, the permanent residents next door, had a lovely sandy beach. Where none had been. He accused them of stealing his sand. Took them to court. Where the Fontaines explained water currents to him. And the value of tree roots for holding things in place.

And the judge explained fines to him.

*O*ur *Summer Home* had a hot tub. It was on the deck, lakeside. The motor was underneath, essentially hanging in mid-air with just enough frame to keep it from dropping onto the ground. That is to say, there was no enclosure, let alone a soundproofed enclosure. The motor was on 24/7. Presumably so the tub was ready to use the minute renters arrived.

There was no way to turn off the motor, from the outside. As the renters at *Tranquility Cottage* discovered. And the renters at *Back to Nature*. And the renters at *TGIF*. Not to mention all of the permanent residents and, eventually, all of the weekenders.

One person thought to turn the temperature down. That would at least reduce how often and for how long the fucking motor was on, right? He discovered that the lowest possible temperature setting was 80 degrees. 80 fucking degrees! He smiled when he thought of the owner's electricity bill, but then got really pissed off because he and people like him were actively trying to reduce their energy use, switching, for example, from a hot water tank to an on-demand system. And here this guy had the godzilla-of-all hot water tanks set to 100 degrees. When no one was even using it. There weren't enough environmentally-conscious people to compensate for such hogs. Not enough Indias to compensate for Canada. So no wonder, the world—

The renters at *Tranquility Cottage*, *Back to Nature*, and *TGIF* sued their rental owners. Said owners had, after all, advertised 'quiet'.

The owners, in turn, sued the owner of *Our Summer Home*.

But first, or in addition (we'll never know), someone had a better idea ... (In fact, it wasn't actually his idea; some guy named 'Bud' sent him a message via the contact form at his *Gone Fishin'* cottage rental page.)

When a 'girls only' reunion of some sort arrived at *Our Summer Home*, late at night, after a too-long drive up from the city, they headed immediately to the hot tub. Aaaaaah. Wonderful, they crooned to each other, sipping glasses of Chardonnay, looking up at the stars, listening to someone's playlist, soft and relaxing ...

After just a few minutes, one of them 'felt something'. Very shortly after, screams broke the sound barrier. Amplified, as they were, by the acoustics of Paradise Lake.

Someone called the O.P.P. Someone else called 9-1-1.

Apparently leeches can survive in hot water. (80 degrees is pushing it, but ...)

In minutes, three of them were on their phones. One called the owner, another called a lawyer, and the other called the Ministry of Natural Resources.

In the meantime, one of the guys from the nearest trailer park wandered over. "I'll take 'em," he said.

"What?"

"I'll take 'em." He nodded to the hot tub. "The fish love 'em."

The woman he spoke to, one of the remaining three, not presently engaged in a hysterical phone conversation, nodded, uncertainly, not quite—

He returned with a pail. Ah. Bait. He reached in and grabbed a squirming mess, a broad grin on his face. One of the women turned away. And retched. Another retched before she turned away. The leeches headed to the novel food source that was drifting down in clumps, surely thinking 'Life doesn't get any better than this'.

When the trailer park guy reached in for another fistful of—everything, she threw up again. He grinned at her. Then swallowed one of the leeches. She put her hand over her mouth and ran.

They found her hours later on the other side of the lake. When she recovered, the women, in a sort of class suit, sued the owner *and* the trailer park guy. For emotional trauma.

Near the end of the summer, everyone at *Back to Nature*, and in the three houses on either side, got sick. What are the odds? Pretty good, actually, when the rental owners don't understand that their septic tanks should be pumped every year. Some of them probably didn't even realize their house *had* a septic tank. Did they think there was a municipal sewage system? No. They just didn't think. Well, did they see any grates or sewer covers on the roads? They didn't look. And those who *did* understand, well, everyone they talked to said that pumping the tank every three to five years is fine. But everyone they talked to had shit from just two or three people going into the tank. Not four times that amount.

The odds are even better because the trailer parks didn't even have septic tanks. They had outhouses. Which were also being overloaded.

The RVs at the trailer parks had inside toilets, but when you have an RV, you're supposed to take your gray and black water to an RV dumping station. Who had the time? It was so much easier to just dump it into the lake.

So. At first, the people who got sick thought it was from swimming in the lake. Because the outhouses were, yes, situated out of sight, but still, within fifty feet from shore. (Because who's going to walk *a hundred feet* to take a shit?) And often uphill from the shore. And certainly upcurrent from someone.

Then people thought it was from the drinking water. Paradise Lake wasn't connected to any municipal water system, of course, so the water that came out of the tap came from a well. A well that pumped up the groundwater into pipes that end in faucets. A well that was right there on the property. In many cases, near the septic tank. And the outhouses. In fact, some of the older weekend cottages still drew their drinking water directly from the lake. As did the trailer parks. (Yes, the RVs at the trailer parks had fresh water tanks, but if they weren't going to the depot to dump their gray and black water tanks, they weren't going to the depot to refill their fresh water tanks.) Which was fine thirty years ago, but not now.

To summarize, because of the rentals and the trailer parks, there was, averaged over the whole year, about five times as much shit finding its way not only into the lake, but also into the groundwater.

So did all those people get sick from swimming in the lake or from drinking out of the tap? Who knew?

Everyone pointed the finger at *Back to Nature*. It was off-grid. But *everyone* at Paradise Lake was off-grid when it came to water and sewage. And *Back to Nature* had a well and a septic system. What set it apart was that it was off-grid when it came to energy; instead of electricity, it used solar and a couple small propane tanks.

So Vic logged on to their listing (as 'Alex Cumming') and sent the owner a picture. Of toilet paper floating in the lake in front of the trailer park which was a few lots upcurrent from their location. She got a close-up of the turd in the middle.

After all the vomiting, and diarrhea, and fevers, and vomiting, and diarrhea had passed, and after all the toilets, sinks, bedding, living room furniture, and curtains had been cleaned (or simply replaced), and after all the deworming meds had done their thing, the lawyers were called.

The renters sued the owners, the owners sued each other and the trailer parks, the residents sued the renters and the owners and the trailer parks, and everyone sued the Township and the Ministry of Natural Resources.

Speaking of the odds, every summer, several renters of *Muskrat Love* got bit.

And every one of *them* sued the Captain and Tennille.

Satan Takes Over

And speaking of *Back to Nature,* in early September, a young woman arrived on a Saturday at 2 p.m. The drive from the city had been long, but uneventful. She unpacked, got settled, read the 'Welcome Packet', made a cup of coffee, then took it onto the deck. She sunk into the lounge chair with a delighted sigh. The sun, the water, the trees … It was wonderful. Just … wonderful.

The power went out at 3 p.m. It didn't affect her, because, as she was well aware, *Back to Nature* was off-grid. In fact, she realized the power had gone out only because she happened to see all the lights go off at once in the houses across the lake.

And because fifteen seconds later, all of the automatic generators at Paradise Lake came on. There were three on her left, two on her right, and five across the lake.

The noise was deafening. (No wonder. Calm water. Loud sound.)

But not as deafening as it was ten minutes later, which was how long it took for the ten manual generators to be turned on. Another three on her left, another two on her right, and another five across the lake.

Yup. Twenty in all. (Small body of calm water. Surrounded by hills.) (The sound was skidding across the water, bouncing off the hills, skidding back, getting amplified each time …)

She tried going out for a paddle, up the river, but two out of every three houses along the river also had generators chugging away.

She tried going for a hike in the forest, and although half an hour in, it was good, every time the path took her up, she'd hear the roar in the distance. What the hell did everyone need a generator for? *All afternoon?* Could they not do without tv and video games for a few hours?

When it started to get dark, she headed back. She figured she could manage until everyone went to bed, and then she'd go for a moonlight paddle. That'd be nice.

So, in the meantime, she put in her earplugs (which she had, because she lived in the city) and went out to the deck again. No. Not enough. She fiddled with their placement, pushing them in further than recommended. Still not enough. Pity she didn't have a pair of noise mufflers, like those worn by guys who operate jackhammers. (Vic would've told her they wouldn't've been enough either, even if combined with earplugs.) (Besides, wearing them felt like your skull was in a vice.)

So she went back inside, made sure all the windows were closed, locked actually, for the tightest possible seal (so much for fresh air, and the loons ...). But even then, her earplugs weren't enough.

How did everyone else stand it? Were they deaf? (Some, the older residents and the noise-addicted men, were, probably, yes, at least partly deaf.) Were they that oblivious to their environment? (Oh, definitely yes.)

Okay, so she'd watch a movie. With her earplugs in and the volume as high as it would go. Ah. Okay. That worked.

At midnight, generators were still going. What the hell? When did people go to bed here?

At 1 a.m., generators were still going. Why did people need their generators on at one o'clock in the morning? Surely they weren't still watching tv. And even if they were, how did they figure they had the right to keep others awake, nerves shot, just so they could watch whatever-the-fuck they were watching?

At 2 a.m., generators were still going. She— *What in god's name were people*— Ah. Their freezers. Their precious frozen meat, their dead animals, must not thaw. It was bad enough that livestock farming 'necessitated' clearing so much forest, thus hastening global warming, but they had to kill us all this way too? Even from a purely self-centered point of view, surely the price of the generator fuel exceeded the price of however much meat was in their freezer at the time. Could these people not do simple arithmetic?

At 3 a.m., generators were still going. And she was still fuming. She went online (again) to see if there was a time indicated for when the power would be back on. No.

At 4 a.m., she gave up. She left. Went back to the city. It'd be much quieter there.

Having received her email, the owner arrived next day at noon. The power was still out. Twenty generators were still on.

He stomped to the house next door. To ask them to turn off their generator.

No one was home.

He found the switch and turned it off himself.

He went to the next house.

No one was home.

He found the switch and turned it off himself.

He went to the next house.

No one was home.

That one took longer to deal with because it was one of the automatic propane-fuelled generators. Eventually, he just turned off the propane feed.

He carried on to the next house.

No one was home.

What the hell?

At around 4 p.m., just as he'd completed his circuit around the lake, all of the generators he'd turned off were turned back on.

He went back to the house next door. They'd spent the day in the city, shopping. Because, you know, generators can cause quite a racket.

You think?

He reached out and turned off the guy's generator. Again.

The guy looked at him. And turned it back on.

He turned it back off again.

The guy turned it back on. He really didn't get it. But this was his property and his generator, and he had a right to do whatever he wanted on his property with his stuff!

(And at four of the houses, no one had returned from wherever, because no one was there to begin with; the houses were rentals with automatic systems that would turn on whenever the power went out—whether there was anyone there or not—and stay on until the power came back on. Go figure.)

If someone in the city had set up their stereo outside, put on some music, cranked up the volume, then just left, you can bet everyone on the block would be there with golf clubs and baseball bats. What the hell was wrong with people here? Why were the rules different?

No matter. He couldn't expect people to pay $3,000 a weekend or $5,000 a week to stay inside all day with the tv blaring. Or to wander around a shopping mall in the city.

He went back to his cottage and called the O.P.P. Surely this was a noise violation.

No, it wasn't. Noise bylaws were in effect from 11 p.m. to 8 a.m.

"So if it's still going on at 11 p.m., I can call you again? And you'll—"

"No, generators are allowed."

"Why? What—"

"For warmth."

"In August?"

"And cooking."

"At three o'clock in the morning?"

"I don't write the rules."

He hung up.

Then called back.

"Is that the case even when there *isn't* a power outage?"

"Yes, sir."

"So ... people with just trailers ... without hydro hook-up ... "

There was off-grid and there was off-grid ...

He hung up.

Then called back.

"I'd like to report an incident of 'disturbing the peace'."

"There is no 'Disturbing the Peace' law in Ontario."

He hung up. Went online.

Then called back.

"I'd like to report an incident of 'causing a disturbance'."

"That's a federal law. We're the provincial police."

He hung up. And damn near threw his phone through the window.

At 11 p.m., the generators were still going.

What do you need your generator on for at two o'clock in the morning? That's what he asked his other-side next-door neighbour when he banged on their door.

The man who answered the door was confused. *Confused!* "It's an automatic system. It comes on when the power goes out and stays on until it comes back on."

Seriously? He'd never heard of anything so ... *stupid.*

"Isn't there a manual override? The thing has a circuit breaker, doesn't it?"

The man closed his door and went back to bed.

Next day, he called the Township. To propose a noise trespass bylaw.

"Noise bylaws are provincial."

"But municipalities can pass bylaws of their own, right?"

"I suppose."

"You suppose? I'm sorry, I thought I was talking to the Mayor."

"You are."

"Well then, let me tell you how to do your job. You *can* pass bylaws of your own. Many municipalities have, for example, prohibited the use of leaf blowers. You know, those high-pitched whining things—"

"That's different."

"How so?"

"It just is."

Breathe. Just—breathe.

"Generators typically emit noise in the 65 to 80 dB range. Which is *equivalent* to a leaf blower. And there are *twenty* of them in operation as we speak. Here. In your township. On *waterfront* properties. You're aware that sound travels remarkably well across water?"

No response. ('Emit'? 'Equivalent'?)

He hung up. (The Mayor, that is.)

(Well, and then the other guy.)

Who then spent several hours figuring out which Ministry to contact.

Then another couple hours looking for an off-hours phone number.

Then another couple hours writing an email. About the gratuitous use of fossil fuels when we should be reducing ... About the impact on wildlife ... About the analogue of physical trespass ...

When only the first 100 of his carefully-prepared 2684 words got sent via the contact form, he nearly lost it. Again.

Finally, he called his M.P.P.

"It's after midnight."

"Yes," he said cheerfully.

"I was asleep."

"How nice for you!"

"Call the office—"

"You'll want to hear this now," he lied.

The M.P.P. sighed. Go ahead.

"I'd like to propose an amendment to the noise bylaws governing use of generators on waterfront properties. I propose that they must be installed roadside, not lakeside; that they must be installed on soundproof pads; that they must be installed in soundproof enclosures; and that their use be limited to a two-hour window in the morning, say 8 to 10, and another two-hour window in the evening, say 6 to 8. That would enable people to have a cup of coffee (though there are neat little propane burners for that) and a hot shower, to flush their toilets a few times (if they simply cannot haul a pail of water up from the lake), and to recharge their flashlights, cellphones, tablets, laptops, and so on. It would be enough to keep the contents of their refrigerators and freezers from spoiling, and it would be enough to keep their water pipes from freezing. Most people on waterfront properties have outdoor propane grills, so cooking shouldn't be a problem if they can't survive for a few days on food that doesn't require cooking. Most people on waterfront properties also have a woodstove, it's part of the cottage kitsch, so warmth shouldn't be a problem, though I'm open to having one amendment for May to October and another for November to April. There's simply no need," he summarized, "for *anyone's* generator, let alone *twenty people's* generators, to be on *continuously,* all day and all night."

No response. Had the guy fallen asleep?

"Hello?"

"Yeah, sure, put it in writing and send it to me in the morning."

"You'll take it to the legislature or whatever?"

"Hell no, not if it's coming from just one person."

"Oh. Okay, how many signatures do I need?"

"I don't know, I usually just deal with lobbies. At least a thousand?"

"But there are only 200 people here."

"Well, then."

There was a silence. Of disbelief.

"You want *me* to canvas the waterfront property owners in the province?"

"Well, *I'm* not going to do it."

"But don't you think that's your job? To represent your constituents?"

The *M.P.P.* was laughing when he hung up.

So the owner of *Back to Nature* sued the lot of them: every one of the 20 property owners with a generator, the O.P.P., the Township, and Ministry, and his jackass-of-an-M.P.P.

And then ...

By way of context, it used to be that just a few people on the lake were into campfires, and they were up only occasionally. But with the rentals and the trailer parks, and the whole cottage mythos (though if a house with an entertainment center, marble counters, and a hot tub was a cottage, then Vic lived in a shed), a mythos that included having a campfire (despite the obvious: people weren't camping, they were living in a cottage/house), there were campfires at a good ten or fifteen properties. On a regular basis. So now, more often than not, it seemed, certainly more often than was desirable (because there was always just enough wind and it was always blowing toward her end of the lake), smoke drifted onto her property. And stayed there, because of the surrounding forested hills.

And so. Vic headed down to the water one sunny summer day, anticipating the sheer beauty of sparkles on the water, music in her headphones, a cup of tea in her right hand, a good book in her left, the fresh air, and—fuck. Someone had a fire going. She could smell the smoke as soon as she sat down. Instant headache. (From the benzene, formaldehyde, carbon monoxide—she wasn't actually sure which toxic chemical was the headache trigger, but thankfully they weren't migraines, as was the case with some people.) She turned to her right and sure enough, she saw smoke rising from the rental property six lots upwind. It was 11:00 in the morning! Why—

She turned her chair a bit, so her back was to the smoke. Nope.

She put on her smoke mask (not only did she keep one in her kayak for engine fumes, she now kept one down at the water for this very reason ...). Nope.

She tried breathing through her mouth. Nope.

She headed back up to her cabin, made sure all the windows were closed, and settled on her couch.

At 1:00, it was still going strong. Determined to enjoy at least part of the day, she headed out in her kayak. And as she passed the property she saw that *there wasn't even anyone outside enjoying the campfire.* (Though since there weren't any flames, it was hardly a campfire. A smokepit is more like it.)

And that really pissed her off. It was one thing to have to go inside for an hour while someone upwind had a campfire, chatting with friends, maybe toasting marshmallows with the kids. (Though when was the last time you saw kids toasting marshmallow at a campfire? They're inside playing video games or chatting on social media.) That she accepted. It was quite another to have to spend the whole fucking day inside for—what? Because someone mindlessly associates being 'up north at the cottage' with 'campfire'? Even though they're inside, probably watching 'the game' on their huge flat-screen tv?

It occurred to her that maybe they thought the smoke was keeping the mosquitoes away. First, no. That's just another part of the cottage mythos. Second, even if continuous smoke *did* deter mosquitoes, given the resulting 'smoke trespass', it becomes a competing rights issue. And since there are alternative ways to prevent mosquito bites that *don't* involve trespass—a fly swatter, a mosquito zapper, repellent lotions and sprays, a bug hat, jackets, and pants ... What if honking your car horn kept the bugs away? Would it be okay for you to do *that* for 8 hours?

Vic decided that if the smokepit was still going when she returned, she'd stop and say something.

And it was. Still going when she returned. At 7:00 in the evening. And there was *still* no one there, enjoying it. So she lingered at their dock, hoping someone would see her. Sure enough, someone appeared at the door.

"I'd like to talk to you," she called up.

"We're in the middle of dinner," the woman called down.

So? She expects me to sit in my kayak, paddling to stay in one place, until they're done? Or go home and paddle back? She can't stop eating for a minute?

"I'd like you to put out your fire," Vic called up. She added that it had been smoking for eight hours, no one was even enjoying it, there were six houses downwind ...

"I'll do it after dinner," the woman replied, turning away.

No. Her casual response indicated that she hadn't understood the incredible rudeness of her behavior, the utter lack of consideration ...

"No," Vic said emphatically. She'd decided she could be a little more aggressive with asshole *renters* because there was little chance of retaliation—they didn't know where she lived. "Put it out now."

The woman's response was unclear.

"Well, I'll be contacting the owner then," Vic said as she started to paddle away. Hopefully, it would kill their chance to rent again.

"I AM the owner, BITCH!" the woman screamed at Vic.

Oops. Well, even so she probably didn't know where she lived, and worse—

"Then you should know better, you should know that—"

The woman yelled something else that Vic couldn't make out.

"Look, it's not an unreasonable request—"

"Move along!" the woman said then, dismissively, actually shooing Vic away with her fingers. As if she was a child.

Vic did *not* move along.

Next thing she knew, there was a guy running down the hill onto the dock yelling at her. "Why don't you just fuck off and mind your own business!"

"I *am* minding my own business," Vic replied calmly. "When your smoke comes onto my property, it becomes my business."

"You're crazy, you know that?"

No, I'm being extremely rational.

"You're a fucking cunt!" he screamed at her then.

Woh. The guy was *so* angry—

Then another man came down to the dock and identified himself also as the owner. "You've upset my wife," he said matter-of-factly, and, oddly, ignoring the raving lunatic beside him. "We were having dinner."

What? *I've* upset *her*? Because she had to stop eating for a minute? (What *is* it with people and eating food?)

Vic repeated what she'd said about eight hours, downwind, headache, no one's even enjoying it ...

"If you could keep your smoke on your own property, there'd be no problem," she concluded, "but you can't, so—"

"That's scientifically impossible," he said.

Oooh, 'scientifically'. Such a smart man.

"Just think about it," he added, helpfully.

Vic was tempted to scratch her head and look like a complete idiot.

But frankly, she was a bit stunned by their apparent surprise at her request. ('You're crazy!) This was not a new issue. It's why, for example, slaughterhouses and solvent industries are so widely hated. And it's why there are zoning bylaws in so many Townships. (Not in this Township. Of course not.)

"If you can't handle a little smoke," he said then, "just pack up and go home."

"This *is* home. I *live* here."

That also seemed to take him by surprise.

What?

By this time, the other guy was really losing his shit. He was charging the full length of the dock at Vic again and again as if trying to scare away a bear.

"You know what you should do?" He suddenly stopped charging for a minute. But he was practically spitting, he was so excited by what he was about to say. "You should take your headphones off, get some rocks, smash them against your head, then jump in the lake, and drown. Die."

Part of her was thinking, 'That's a lot of words.'

Another part of her was thinking, 'I already have my headphones off.'

Yet another part of her was thinking, 'That's a hair away from a death threat.'

So she moved along.

Vic was no stranger to sexism: as a female human being, she'd been ignored, dismissed, and/or insulted all her life. This was not even the first time she'd experienced such ... fury. In fact, including the ATV guy and the rock pile guy, it was ... the sixth time. Assuming one man per house, that's six out of thirty, which is one in five. One in five men had responded with absolute outrage, two practically foaming at the mouth, when she'd challenged them on something. That in itself isn't particularly new. Someone once said that "When men make demands, they expect women to comply." True enough. And when women make demands, men completely lose their shit.

No, what caught her by surprise was the vehemence of the response, so disproportionate to the stimulus (two of the six had uttered near death threats), and the ease with which those who called her a cunt did so (three of the six).

On top of all that, in four of the six cases, she'd been significantly older than the man in question. Insults among peers is one thing, but it takes a certain arrogance to insult so shamelessly someone twenty or thirty years your senior: no deference, no hesitation, they were just as reckless, just as abusive, with Vic as she imagined they might be with their peers.

Satan Takes Over

What was going on? Yes, our society has become increasingly uncivil. And some have attributed that to the internet: in general, people are more insulting when they are anonymous and, no surprise, that rudeness eventually becomes a habit and crosses over into 'real' life. Or maybe it's the influence of the tv shows people watch or, especially in the case of the men, the video games they play. In retrospect, Vic thought, it's unlikely the guy on the dock came up with hitting her face with rocks and drowning on his own. It was just so weird and specific.

But that doesn't explain the sexual nature of the insults. Or the ease—and the rage—with which she was called a bitch or a cunt.

So she thought it could be due not to the internet per se, but to internet *porn*. Most porn, now, is incredibly aggressive and humiliating to women (she'd read Dines' *Pornland* and Bray and Reist's *Big Porn, Inc.*): women are routinely slapped, hit, fucked; spat on, pissed on; and yes, of course, called a bitch and a cunt. *Routinely*. And most men watch porn. We become what we expose ourselves to. Therefore, most men will think they have the right to hurl abuse, sexual abuse, at a woman. Any woman. Anytime. Anywhere. (Women: act accordingly.)

So, how *should* Vic have dealt with the problem? Well, first, she shouldn't've been a woman.

And second, she—no, actually, that's it. If a man, greying at the temples, had stopped on his way past, she suspected the whole interaction would've unfolded quite differently.

By way of conclusion, the next time a smokepit sent smoke her way, she (well, a 'Jerry Bentham') sent an email to the owner of the property immediately downwind of the smokepit, whose current renters must have surely been suffering even more than she.

As it turned out, he'd been receiving complaints (and requests for refunds) because the cottage reportedly smelled like smoke and it was advertised as being smoke-free. Each time, he'd accused the previous renters of smoking inside the cottage, but they all insisted they had not done so and, further, said they'd noticed the smell as well. (Vic was surprised they couldn't tell the difference between cigarette smoke and wood smoke, but then Shoogles was surprised *she* couldn't tell the difference between dead rabbit smell and dead squirrel smell.) (She was also surprised they didn't just *see* the smoke, but then it occurred to her that there had been gaps between renters, and the regular cleaners had been leaving the bathroom window open—which happened to face upwind—to air out the space.)

Three times he'd had to hire, at great expense, special cleaners to wipe down the ceiling and the walls—every surface, actually—with an odour-absorbing solution, shampoo the rugs, have the curtains dry-cleaned, launder all the bedding and towels ... (Vic could have told him it would still take a couple weeks for the smell to disappear ...)

In her email, Vic explained what was happening—mystery solved!—and suggested that perhaps a demonstration was needed, since a mere discussion was inadequate. If, she wondered, someone upwind of the smokepit rental were to spray paint their outdoor chairs one breezy afternoon ...

So the downwind owner contacted an upwind owner, who readily agreed to co-operate, because he'd had a problem with an upwind smokepit as well ... so if this worked, maybe he'd contact the next upwind owner ...

Well. Vic didn't realize there were industrial pressurized spray machines. (She'd been imagining a small spray paint can from the local hardware store.)

And hats off to whoever thought to use neon pink.

Downwind, where the smokepit was, the adults became dizzy (the guy had used an oil or acrylic-based paint, the kind with all the warnings about needing proper ventilation during use) and the kids became brain-damaged (not that anyone would know).

But it was the next occupants who posted feedback on the rental webpage. About how strange it was that everything on one side of the property—not only the grill and some pails and rakes, but also the screens, the windows, even the siding—seemed to have been covered by a fine mist of spray paint. Pink spray paint.

(The previous occupant hadn't noticed the pink on his pick-up until he got home. AND HE'S GONNA FUCKING KILL THE GUY WHO DID THAT!) (Just as soon as he figures out WHO did that.)

When the owner read the post, he flew his jet in—well he would've if jets had been able to land—oh god, don't even go there—and had everything repainted that afternoon. (Where *do* these people get all their money from?)

A lake-wide paintball war ensued. (Don't ask. There's simply no logical explanation.)

And yet. It happened again. One smokepit. Two smokepits. Three ...

First, due to the mild breeze, the combined smoke of ten smokepits spread out across the lake and by 3 p.m., everyone's property had been invaded.

Then because the breeze stopped, the smoke just sort of sat there. (Remember, the whole lake was surrounded by forested hills.) By 4 p.m., Paradise Lake was a sink full of smoke.

There was an older couple renting on the lake. They'd both contracted COVID, had been hospitalized, and had recovered, though they would have respiratory difficulties for the rest of their lives. To celebrate the fact that they'd survived, they splurged for a week on Paradise Lake. But their cottage wasn't one of the super-sealed luxury rental homes, so they'd watched the approaching smoke with a great deal of trepidation. And now it was causing them some distress. They didn't exert themselves. They did their breathing exercises. They took their medications.

In the meantime, a middle-aged couple and their daughter were staying at a nearby rental. The daughter had asthma. They'd brought an air purifier, and it was set on high. They'd brought her inhaler, but it was almost empty. They'd also brought her rescue inhaler, but two puffs every four hours didn't seem like enough.

Both the older couple and the father had asked their next-door neighbours to put out their smokepits. In response, they'd increased the smoke by piling on wet wood.

Everyone on the lake had a headache. Well, except for those who didn't have that part of the brain that *gets* a headache from toxic smoke.

At 5 p.m., the older couple gave up and called an ambulance.

Within an hour, it was almost there. Almost. A few minutes after it had turned onto Paradise Lake Road, an ATV ran into it. And then the second ATV ran into the first, and the third ran into the second, and ... You get the picture. Who'd've anticipated that an ATV would be racing down the *middle* of the road? Let alone ten of them? (Vic would have.) (But not, alas, the ambulance driver.)

(When they sued—the ATVs, that is—their lawyer argued that if the ambulance driver hadn't've had the siren going, she would've heard the roar of the ATVs and been able to pull over to the side of the road.)

At 6 p.m., the middle-aged couple and their daughter got into their car. They planned to drive into town, hoping to find an open pharmacy. Failing that, they'd continue up to the city, perhaps straight to Emerg. They didn't make it to the main road, let alone the highway.

"I have to stay here," the ambulance driver said to the father, nodding to her unconscious colleague in the passenger seat. She pointedly did not nod to any of the ATV drivers strewn on the road. "He's stable now, but—"

"I understand."

"You've got a rescue inhaler?"

"Yes, but—"

She nodded. "Okay, best you go straight to Emerg. Turn around, get in a boat, and head up the river to the airport. I'll call and have a medical helicopter meet you there."

"Thank you." He quickly headed back to his car.

"I was on my way to 18 Sunset Lane," she called out after him.

He turned.

"There's an older couple there ... Can I tell them to get down to their dock if they can and wait for you there?"

He nodded.

Fortunately, the rental came with a boat, but pontoon boats are not known for their speed. Which, given the visibility—or lack thereof—was probably just as well. And at least there would be room for the five of them.

As they slowly approached the dock at 18 Sunset Lane, they saw the older couple waiting as directed. Each was hugging an oxygen tank. The parents exchanged a tentative smile; maybe their daughter could get a puff if things got really bad.

A few minutes later, as the boat puttered along through the smoke, they realized their mistake: they'd've been better off waiting inside a cottage for a second ambulance. Should they turn back or keep going? Maybe they could stop at the next occupied cottage?

They were just about to round the point into the cove at which the lake became the river when a jetslam slammed into them. He hadn't seen them because of the smoke. (Right. *That's* why.)

The jetslammer flew over the boat. And landed on a pile of rocks.

A moment later, the impact ignited the oxygen tanks.

Someone renting at the cove heard the explosion and called 9-1-1.

Meanwhile, at 4 p.m., the Sullivans, who typically kept their eyes glued to the tv (and their backs to the lake), looked outside. And panicked. Understandably so. All afternoon, they'd been seeing air quality alerts and haze warnings on the weather channel, because of uncontrolled forest fires in the northwest part of the province. What they saw out their window was considerably more than haze. The fires were spreading! They'd be at Paradise Lake soon!

They started packing for evacuation, stuffing their RV full of food and water (certainly), mementos (of course), clothing (yes), their meds (yes!), but also their 72" flat screen tv, their weed trimmer, the contents of the kitchen cupboards, the contents of the basement workshop, the paintings on their living room wall, especially the one of the dogs playing poker and the black velvet Elvis ...

By 7 p.m., some of the smokepits had been turned into bonfires. Because, hey, we're at the cottage!

At 8 p.m., the wind picked up. Someone called the fire department. Because, hey, we're all going to die!

The fire truck collided with the RV, which was going faster than—well, faster than it should have been going, period. But especially on a gravel road and especially when driven by someone over eighty.

The second fire truck couldn't get past until the RV tow truck from the city arrived.

Charges were laid. For leaving a campfire unattended, reckless discharge of a weapon (the paintball gun), assault, failure to give right of way to emergency vehicles, reckless driving, driving under the influence, driving without a license, operating a PWC over 10kmh within 100' of the shore ...

And suits were filed—by and against residents, renters, owners, the Township, the Fire Department, and the Ministries of Natural Resources, the Environment, Transportation, Health, and Justice. For misrepresentation, loss of income, unreasonable interference with use and enjoyment of land, failure to prevent odour discharge causing an adverse effect, trespass of a noxious substance, contaminant migration, harassment, property damage, personal injury, unreasonable conduct ...

And that did it. Something had to be done. It was the last straw. The one that broke— Actually, contrary to the featured event at the Canadian-American Days in Myrtle Beach, camels are *not* common in Canada. It was the last *fly*— blackfly, deerfly, horsefly, hell, could've been just a housefly— Regardless, it was the one that made the moose lose its mind. (Whereupon, bellowing, it thundered onto the nearest dock and plunged antlers-first into the water.)

That is to say, after a year of this shit (i.e., lawsuits), the Township (per a suggestion sent to them by a 'J. Jack Rousseau') got together with the three surrounding Townships, all of which had been experiencing the same thing—a huge influx of absentee landlords with 100% occupancy of 'sleeps twelve' rental houses, and trailer parks appearing overnight like mushrooms, and long-time residents none too pleased ...

Together, they applied for and received legal jurisdiction over all bodies of water and all Crown land within their boundaries. (Honestly, the various Ministries sighed with relief at this request.)

Then they took an inventory of their lakes and did some zoning, essentially dividing their lakes into three categories: quiet refuge, family fun, party place.

Then they got busy and increased their bylaw coverage (and clarity), their bylaw enforcement, and their bylaw fines.

The smaller lakes, like Paradise Lake, were declared quiet refuge zones. So no screaming kids, no loud parties, no motorized vehicles on the water or the trails (to be clear—no jetslams, or jetboards, and no motor boats of any kind or size for any purpose; no ATVs, no snowmobiles). This left a great number of trails for hiking, snowshoeing, and skiing. As a bonus, the Township lay down dirt wherever the rocks and roots, exposed by continuous ATV use, made walking difficult. (After all, they'd been laying down gravel on the roads for decades for the heavy logging trucks and dump trucks, the latter from the quarry.) This meant no more walking in fume trails, no more scurrying to get out of the way, no more looking at your feet the whole way so you don't trip or twist an ankle, no more detouring around path-wide mud-sucking puddles! It also meant that many sections of the official snowmobile/ATV trail system of had to have detours made. (Yup. They'd been within hearing distance of now 'quiet refuge' lakes. Who knew?)

These lakes tended to have a relatively healthy ecosystem (a pair of loons, some ducks, geese, and even herons, lots of beaver, a few otters …), so they decided to try and keep them that way. No fishing allowed. No hunting allowed. The provincial noise bylaw, created with urban areas in mind that had a higher level of background or ambient noise, and no bodies of water that would increase transmission distance and volume, was strengthened considerably for these lakes. Even the noise of maintenance and minor renovations was limited to certain hours on certain days. (And if you had to be somewhere else during those time periods, well, hire a high school student or a fixed pension retiree to do the work.) All outdoor lighting was prohibited. Flashlights with rechargeable batteries were provided.

No potato cannons. Ever.

No fireworks. Ever.

As for the gun club and its shooting range, the Township ordered an acoustic audit. And yeah. It should never have been located where it was. The club was presented with three options:

1. Move. There was a great spot out on the multi-laned highway, between the Big-Trucks-With-out-Mufflers repair shop and Jackhammers-R-Us.

2. Put the whole thing underground—ten levels underground—in a bunker.

3. Have members use silencers. (Slight problem: they're illegal in Canada. Easy solution: apply for an exception and require members to leave their silencers at the club in a lockbox.)

And the gun club/shooting range wasn't the only one. There were other businesses near other (now) quiet refuge lakes that, due to not only an acoustic audit, but also an environmental audit, had to relocate or implement several modifications.

The medium-sized lakes, especially those with a naturally sandy shore, were designated for family fun. Again, no jetslams, and no cigarette boats; motorboats were allowed, but constrained by size and a speed limit. ATVs and snowmobiles allowed, but only on the designated trails. (This left several trails for hiking, snowshoeing, and skiing, which were also resurfaced.) Recreational (and other) noise was allowed from nine in the morning to nine at night. Outdoor lighting fixtures had to have a full top shade, so the light shone directly down (for safe navigation of paths). No potato cannons. No fireworks except on province-wide holidays. No killing animals except in self-defence.

The larger lakes were the party places. They had the physical room for the (relatively) safe operation of jetslams and cigarette boats; they also had (more) acoustic space for engine noise and loud music (both of which would dissipate somewhat before reaching people sitting on their docks) (who, in any case, might enjoy said engine noise and loud music). As a bonus, the Townships jointly established two racetracks, one on water (on the largest of the party place lakes) and one on land (adjacent to another of the party place lakes). The one was near a quarry operation, and the other was near a logging operation, so there was already almost-constant noise in the area that exceeded 120dB (the pain and danger threshold). Neither had, now, any wildlife nearby or any permanent residences nearby. On all of the party place lakes, no bylaws applied. That's right, people: *anything goes.* (Well, except for stuff prohibited by provincial and federal laws.)

Speaking of which, several Ministries, provincial and federal, scrambled to review their existing laws (which were to be considered additional to any Township laws covering Crown land and water), and they tweaked a few. Most notably, the one that said people could start a fire anywhere, anytime. The law now said that all outdoor fires (including sky lanterns) were banned: the traditional campfire belonged to a bygone era in which one, they were actually necessary, and two, they were understood to occur only at actual campsites, not at houses, situated a hundred feet apart. It helped that another wildfire, this one northeast of the region, had occurred that summer, and that a new hire at the Ministry of Natural Resources informed everyone there about the relationship between global warming and forest fires (that is, he screamed at them that forest fires were going to increase in frequency and severity *without* the help of campfires).

Generators were allowed on waterfront properties, but only according to a comprehensive and well-thought-out proposal put forth by the region's M.P.P., specifying that they be placed roadside, on a soundproof pad, and in a soundproof enclosure, and that their use be limited to one morning and one evening two-hour window and (This proposal was highlighted as forward-looking in his upcoming, and successful, campaign for re-election.)

No trailer parks were allowed on any waterfront. (Nor dumpsters, nor shipping containers.)

A septic system was a prerequisite for *any* habitation on waterfront.

No more Crown land was to be sold for development. In fact, no more development was allowed. (The forementioned new hire had read Kim Stanley Robinson's *Ministry for the Future* and was familiar with E. O. Wilson's *Half-Earth* Project ...) The Crown bought back all as-yet-undeveloped lots.

Lastly, a surtax, payable to the Townships, was levied on waterfront rental properties, calculated on a per renter per day basis, to take into account the additional stress on the ecology, the roads, the dumps, and so on.

Even so, the absentee landlords were happy. They had to adjust their advertising accordingly, but all of them still had something wonderful with which to attract renters. This surprised the hell out of Vic until she discovered that many of them had *several* rental properties and had ended up with at least one quiet refuge to rent, one family fun cottage to rent, and one party place to rent. Some emphasized that in the one case, their advertised peace and quiet was actually guaranteed by Township laws, and in the other, that partiers would not be disturbed by irate neighbours calling the police ...

Satan Takes Over

When all was said and done, some of the permanent residents and weekenders found themselves on the 'wrong' lake, but the Townships co-operated to facilitate trade sales. For those whose cottage had been in the family for years, this wasn't a great solution, but truth be told, it was better than the alternative; many had been just about to sell anyway.

So ... everyone lived happily ever after.

And Vic didn't have to rent out her beloved cabin after all.